NIFFIN

RENATA DAWN

Cover Design: by Karen McKinney

Published by Strolling Donkeys, LLC, 30 N Gould St STE N, Sheridan, WY 82801

WWW.strollingdonkeys.com

Our mission is to help readers understand the importance of a personal relationship with Jesus Christ.

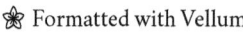 Formatted with Vellum

To Jesus Christ, for always being the hero in my story.

CHAPTER 1

Navajo Indian Reservation, 1962

*T*he dread creeps up on him slowly, steady as dust settles over that all-too-familiar stretch of desert road. The air thickens with lament, anguish clawing at him at the mere thought of her. Time twists here —it feels like yesterday, feels like ages ago, speeding by and stalling all at once. He's trapped in a self-made prison, shackled to what was, refusing to allow the new into his life, bound to what could have been.

A memory flickers, faint as an old photograph yet sharp in its edges: a young woman twirling under the summer sun, long wavy brunette hair catching the light amongst the blue flowers blooming stubbornly in the desert. She's alive in a long, colorful dress, her smile shouting her love for nature, for summer, for whoever's watching her dance. She radiates contentment, carefree and joyful where she is and who she's with.

But the memory quickly sours. His chest knots as the blissful dream suddenly shifts into nightmare. Bitter melancholy gnaws at him as he stares at the cracked earth. Her heart is broken from betrayal, loss—scars enduring long beyond the grave. His passion and love twisted into hate, a sharp need to wipe her out entirely. As he turns away, she fades, dust swirling in the wind, gone as if she was never even there.

——

Pelican's Cove, Florida, 1992

I step into the garden in front of my house, roses and hibiscus bushes brushing the air with their sweet, thick scent. Birds chirp overhead, squirrels rustle, and it's calm—mostly. My favorite spot is the birdbath in the middle, a cement tree with a bowl perched high, etched with birds in flight or resting on branches. But a prickling feeling creeps in, like eyes I cannot see boring into me.

Behind it looms the house, a dark violet Victorian home hugged by woods. Its white front porch glints with elaborate balusters and lace brackets, guarding two violet doors with oval glass panes and heavy brass knobs. Bay windows stack up the right side, showing off the spiraling staircase inside, with a dining room window glowing beside them. Three stories high, the house has been ours since Great-Grandmother Beatrice built it in the 1920s, passing it down like a secret I'm still piecing together. A covered porch juts off the kitchen side, potted flower plants lining the edge where the sun can spill over them. Two sets of white wrought iron tables and chairs, each with yellow seat cushions, sit there invitingly. Beyond, a river laps at the boat dock, steady and quiet.

Mom's voice cuts through, calling me for dinner. A crow caws, sharp and sudden, and I jump. It's perched on the porch railing, huge, with bluish-green eyes that don't look like they belong on any bird. It stares, unblinking, peeling me open—like it knows something I don't like; it's tied to me somehow. My skin crawls as I climb the steps. The crow just sits there still as stone as I slip inside.

The foyer's oak floor gleams under a gold chandelier, the winding staircase curving right. French doors with sheer purple curtains open to the living room—dark green Victorian couches on a multicolor floral rug, a mahogany coffee table between them. Against the back wall, two armchairs flank a mahogany lamp stand with a Tiffany lamp, its stained glass blooming colors. More French doors with green curtains lead to a veranda.

An upright oak piano stands against the floral wallpaper, pink and purple flowers climbing the wall.

I head for the dining room through another set of French doors, cream curtains swaying. The mahogany table seats eight, its cream chairs stitched with grapes and pears. A mahogany china cabinet towers behind, stuffed with Beatrice's crystal wine glasses and serving dishes. "Bernadette!" Mom snaps again, loud and sharp. She's

at the table's end, stern as ever. Cherie slumps beside her, sandy blonde hair rippling with her annoyed huff. "Now we can finally eat," she says, eyeing the salad and spaghetti as if I'm the reason she's so hungry.

"Where's dad?" I ask. Mom's frown deepens.

"Working late at the store again," she says, folding her hands for grace. We start eating in silence, dishes passing without a word. I break it, blurting out what I saw—the crow's weird eyes, its unblinking stare. Cherie's blue eyes slice into me, sharp with doubt.

"Crows don't have eyes like that," she says with a smirk. "And they don't stare at people." I shrug, letting it go for now, but her disbelief stings, like always.

Dinner's done, and I slip through another French door into the kitchen. It's a big room with oak cabinets, an oak floor, and a large island in the middle. Bay windows with red drapes frame a breakfast, and purple cushions soft against the oak bench. The back stairs call, their lavender walls guiding me, and oak banisters lining the second-floor hall. Portraits of dead relatives stare from gold frames, their eyes following me to the third floor.

The tower room's a library now, white paneling and oak floors clashing with the house's old soul. Tall white bookcases line the walls, and five windows with sheer white curtains letting in soft light: two blue recliners beckon, each with an oak end table. I sink into mine—Cherie's is opposite, her sketchpad untouched—and Janis, our little Yorkshire terrier, hops up beside me. I've always liked Mom's name, Jacqueline, and Cherie's, too, better than mine. Dad's name is Bernard—mine's just a clunky echo. Tiredness begins to pull at me, and I head down to my room, Janis trailing. Suddenly, I feel it again—the prickling feeling that someone's watching me. I flick on the staircase light, hurrying down the hall.

I pass the old grandfather clock. It's nine o'clock. I rush toward the last

3

door on the right and rush inside. My room's dark but familiar—green floral quilt on a pine bed, dresser, desk to the left, nightstand with a pink lamp to the right. A big window with matching curtains glows faintly. I flop down on my bed. I can hear the wind blowing against the window. Janis curls up beside me, and sleep overtakes me quickly.

Janis' scratching jolts me awake. I let her out, then shuffle to the kitchen. It's empty, but there are still traces of breakfast—toast out, a pan in the sink. I pour some cereal, eating at the nook, and staring out the bay window. Janis barks, and I grab some orange juice from the fridge. It tips as I set it on the island, juice spilling everywhere. I freeze, staring at the mess, just as Mom storms in. She scolds me for my clumsiness while brushing her dark, wavy hair away from her eyes. She's dressed in a crisp green blouse, white pants, a gold belt, and matching heels. "Get ready," she snaps. "We're going to the store with Cherie."

I trudge upstairs, swapping my slept-in clothes for overalls, a purple short-sleeved shirt, and tan sandals. I snag my amethyst ring from my pink jewelry box, catching my reflection—dark wavy hair like Mom's, brown eyes, pale, freckled skin. Cherie's prettier, taller, olive-toned. In the living room, she's waiting in a pink sundress, curls tight, gold necklace glinting. Mom hustles us out, Janis barking faintly. I hear footsteps echoing from the kitchen—impossible, with us all here. "Did you hear that?" I whisper to Cherie. She frowns, shaking her head. We pile into Mom's brown station wagon and peel off down the forest road.

I watch the forest pass by on the winding road. We cross a bridge. The lake below shimmers, mirroring the trees along its bank. I feel so at peace in nature and would stay in the forest all day if I could. Two black horses catch my eye, frolicking in a field. I want one so badly, and I have a name all picked out: Blessing.

Pelican's Cove rolls into view—a beach town, bungalow shops, salt air. We park at the grocery store, and I step out, the crowd buzzing. I head toward the store, looking back, when I realize my family isn't walking beside me. Mom adjusts her purse and says something to Cherie, but I'm too far ahead to hear it. Suddenly, a blonde guy with striking bluish-green eyes brushes past, muttering to himself, clearly upset. He nearly bumps into me, then chuckles, grinning.

"Hey," I say tentatively. He freezes, staring like I've stunned him, then asks my name. "Bernadette," I tell him. He asks where he can find me, but I don't answer—his mouth doesn't move when he talks, and that's wrong. Why doesn't it move? Mom calls me back. I glance at her, then back at him —he's gone, vanished. I try to shake it off and hurry back to the car, but those eyes linger in my mind, watching still

CHAPTER 2

Phoenix, Arizona, 1924

A young lady, maybe seventeen, spins in the sunshine, a smile breaking wide as summer hums around her. Her long dress flares —vibrant stripes and floral patterns intertwining—a silver angel pendant glinting at her throat, a childhood gift from her father. Dark hair spills straight from under a cowboy hat. The desert stretches beneath her feet: cliff mountains rising, cactus blossoms flaring pink and red, purple wild-flowers hugging the riverbank. She's radiant, oblivious to it, though her energy draws all eyes. He noticed her then, all those years ago, and now clutches that necklace in his hands, the sadness rolling over him.

Summer's flying by, and today I'm off to the movies with Megan. Mom drops us at the theater, waving as she pulls away. I smile back. I love this place—an old building on Pelican's Cove's beach strip, tan stucco and Georgian lines framing the salty hum of Main Street.

Megan's a bundle of light with curly brown hair, olive skin, blue eyes in a round face. She's short, not slim but not heavy, sweet until crossed, then hard as steel. We stride up to the theater, the double-sided sign flashing today's films and promo posters plastering the walls. Inside, a long hallway stretches to the concession stand—red carpet, more posters. My eyes wash over the gleaming red tile, the popcorn maker humming to the left and a drink machine gurgling to the right. We order medium drinks and small popcorns, planning ice cream after.

Megan's in an olive-green shirt and jean skirt, tan sandals showing her gold shell bracelet—I've always wanted one. I'm in a hot pink and navy striped shirt, jean shorts, and a pair of sandals too. We climb to the second floor—my favorite theater—turning left at the landing. It's a dim room, wide with twelve rows. Megan picks a couple of seats back center, and we settle in to watch an action comedy. Her laughter fills the air, and as I listen I'm sure we could be friends forever.

The movie ends, and we spill out onto the beach strip as dusk creeps in. My watch tells me that Mom will soon be here. The warm air's a relief after hours in the chilly theater. I'm debating ice cream when I spot Tony—my crush, as well as the neighborhood clown. His brunette hair ripples in the breeze, his blue eyes bright against a gray shirt, black shorts, and tennis shoes. He's tall, slim, and waving as he closes in. Megan watches me play it cool, but my heart's racing.

Time slows to a crawl. Tony's smile flashes—perfect teeth—and he speaks. I brace for a "hi," nerves buzzing, but he grins and says, "Excuse me, do you have any grey poupon your hair?" I blink, confused. Megan cracks up—*grey poop on your hair*. Tony keeps walking, smirking. I glance back; he's looking, too, then turns away.

"I wanted memorable," I mutter.

"Oh," says Megan, giggling, "that was."

We reach the ice cream shop; its freezer displays are brimming with luscious goodies. Megan picks cookies and cream while I grab a mint chocolate chip, both in waffle cones. We wander, window-shopping beach clothes and trinkets, until Mom pulls up. "How was the movie?"

I dodge the whole subject of Tony, nudging the conversation to next week's beach trip. Megan lets it slide. When we arrive at her grey brick Tudor, she hops out, waving through the open garage.

Back home, I climb the kitchen stairs, Janis trotting behind. I hear mumbled whispers drifting from the library—male voices, low and odd. My pulse races—robbers? I creep up, steps creaking. At the top, heart pounding, I peer inside—nothing. Empty. I shake it off, confused, and head to my room for the night. Somehow, my mind turns off, and sleep overtakes me.

As the morning light filters in, I pull on a red shirt, jean shorts, and white sandals. Downstairs, Janis waits patiently as I pour cereal into a blue bowl. A note says Mom and Cherie are gardening, so I step outside with Janis. They're not there, so I wander to the boat dock, the water lapping gently. And then I feel it again, the prickles. I'm being watched. Janis barks wildly at the kitchen porch. There's nothing there, but now she's hiding behind me and whimpering. I scoop her up, bolting inside.

The kitchen door won't lock—the knob turns, but it sticks. Frantic and scared, I hear knocking on the glass. I peek through the red curtains— nobody. Janis growls. A second knock, then a third, but there's still nothing there. I wrestle the lock shut, panting, then hear pounding—Cherie's fist. I fling the door open. She and Mom are casually standing there. "Where were you?" I blurt out.

"Neighbors," I ask if they saw anyone outside, but Mom says no, eyeing me quizzically. I turn and climb the stairs. As I head toward my room, I see that Beatrice's portrait is crooked. She was so beautiful—dark eyes, curly hair, a white satin dress on a pink chaise. Navajo and Spanish, Mom says, but she's always secretive about her family and her life growing up.

Mom calls me back down to the kitchen. "Were you walking on the handrail outside?" she asks crossly. I'm confused. Mom says there are foot- prints on the porch railing, cigarette butts scattered around. I shake my head.

"No. None of that's mine," I stammer. Just then, Cherie walks in. Mom lets the conversation drop and suggests we take a walk. We take the forest path—ten acres of thick green trees. Birds sing happily while Janis chases squirrels. Mom talks to us about plans for the beach with Megan.

Back home, we play Monopoly at the kitchen table. The strange events from earlier fade from my mind as I enjoy this time with my family. Dad arrives and surprises us with a pizza. Mom looks at him lovingly. His tan khakis and blue polo shirt smell of the store, but he's grinning, pouring tea as Mom dishes out the slices. I ask about a horse for the hundredth time—or at least riding lessons. My dad does own a feed store, after all. Mom agrees that lessons are a good idea, and he promises I can start soon.

Night settles in. So many good things today, but those whispers linger.

CHAPTER 3

A young lady strolls through town, sunlight glinting off Model T Fords and horse-drawn buggies in the Arizona heat. Her black cloche hat blooms with white roses, framing a drop-waist dress—black with a white band and collar, ruffles cascading to her waist. Short black gloves and T-strap heels click as she crosses the dusty road. A blonde man with deep bluish-green eyes leans against a car, his grey pinstripe suit sharp. He tips his fedora, smiling. She meets his gaze, curious, a spark flickering between them in the dry air.

The beach trip's finally here. Megan's meeting me at a diner for lunch, and then we're off to the public beach. I'm dressed in a navy blue short-sleeve shirt, faded jean shorts, and a one-piece bathing suit underneath, with a tan straw hat and beach bag slung over my shoulder—towel, sunglasses, sunscreen tucked inside. Mom drops me off at the diner, a retro fifties hangout with white walls, tiled accents, and a neon hamburger sign glowing out front. Inside, turquoise booths line the right wall, counter stools stretch along the left, and the black-and-white checkerboard floor shines under bright overhead lights.

I settle at the counter, placing my beach bag on the stool beside me, and wait, watching people come and go. Ten minutes pass, and then Megan's mom's black Mercedes pulls up outside. Megan strides in, smiling wide, and takes the seat to my right. She's wearing a light blue shirt, jean shorts, a yellow swimsuit peeking out beneath, and white sandals that click softly on the floor. We order cheeseburgers, fries, and chocolate milkshakes. The waitress, a middle-aged woman with a quick smile, asks if we're splitting the bill. Megan hands her a twenty, grinning. "My treat," she says. I thank her, and she shrugs it off, easy as ever, her laid-back charm lighting up the moment.

We finish eating and head out, slipping on sunglasses, turning right toward the beach—past little shops with colorful awnings, over a wooden bridge creaking underfoot, down sandy stairs to the shore. I picked a spot near a family with camping chairs and a radio playing soft tunes, not too crowded. The music's okay, but I'd rather hear the waves crashing and gulls calling overhead. After slathering on sunscreen, we sit and watch. Teens are tossing a Frisbee nearby, laughing loudly. A dad cracks open a Coke, the fizzy sound tempting in the heat. Megan nods toward a vending machine down the beach, and we walk over, sand warm under our feet. I spot Tony ahead, gazing at me across the dunes. He waves; I wave back, my heart skipping a beat. He casually strolls over, asking where we're headed. "Coke machine," I say, keeping my voice light. He tags along, his hands stuffed in his pockets.

Tony buys us Cokes. We turn and head back to our spot by the water, icy cans sweating in the sun. He sits cross-legged on the sand, tossing a Frisbee my way. I catch it clumsily, throw it back, and we laugh. Megan joins in, and soon, we're knee-deep in the ocean, tossing it around as waves lap at our legs, cool and salty against our skin. My watch says we're fifteen minutes late for pickup—the time slipped away in all the fun.

We say goodbye to Tony, his blue eyes lingering on me as he nods. He seems disappointed. We rush back to the diner, sandals slapping the pavement. I glance back; he's still watching, then turns away, black trunks stark against his tanned skin.

Our moms' cars are waiting, parallel parked along the curb. They're chatting as we load up our bags. I thank Megan's mom, Gloria, for lunch. She smiles at me warmly. "Oh, it's nothing, dear." Mom suggests I treat next time—Megan waves it off, insisting it's no big deal. We say goodbye and head home.

By the time we arrive, I'm tired and thirsty. I pour myself some cold water from a jug in the kitchen before trudging up the back stairs to my room. Sun-soaked, I flop onto the bed and quickly fall asleep, the day's warmth pulling me into happy unconscious.

In my dream, there's a man. He's robbing a woman, stealing her jewelry in a dark, unfamiliar house. I can't see their faces, but I can feel his intent. He wants to hurt her—and he knows her home as if it were his own. A sudden noise startles him. He breaks a window, cuts himself on the jagged glass as he escapes, hides the jewelry, and bleeds out slowly in the shadows.

I wake, heart pounding, an urge to help that woman tugging at me, but I have no idea where to even start. Groggy, I shuffle to the library, hoping dinner's soon so I can shake off the dream and the residual unease. That watched feeling creeps in again—new these past few weeks, sharper now. I grab my book from the shelf, sensing something close, and hurry downstairs to the kitchen. I step out on the porch for some fresh air.

The breeze clears my head, cool against my skin as it rustles the trees. I walk along the forest trail for thirty minutes, turning back as dusk falls, shadows stretching long across the path. When I reach the boat dock, a shadowy figure turns toward me. I can feel negative energy pulsing like a warning through the stillness. I take off running, slowing at the porch stairs, suddenly feeling foolish—then trip. A shadowy hand grips my ankle, five fingers, long nails digging in cold and hard. I kick it off, screaming as it releases me with a faint hiss. The shadowy figure stares up at me, tilting its head slowly, its long hair rippling in an eerie way in the fading light. Mom opens the door and tells me to come inside.

Breathlessly, I blurt out what just happened. Baffled, she tells me it's all my imagination. "No, it's a monster!" I cry, my voice shaking. She quiets me, unconvinced, ushering me inside. It's gone when I look back, but I'm deeply rattled.

Unsteadily, I head upstairs and change into a floral shirt, yellow shorts, and white sandals. With a heavy breath, I head back down for spaghetti. The family chats around the dining table—Mom, Cherie, and Dad swapping stories as usual, as if everything is normal. After cleanup, I peek outside—

nothing but stillness and dark beyond the glass. Janis growls low, barking sharply at the door, and I shut it fast, taking her upstairs with me.

The dream—I look, and my amethyst ring's missing from my jewelry box. I wore it yesterday, I'm sure of it. The monster is real. It can touch me and take things. I try to distract myself, sitting down to read in the library, the lamp glowing steady. But I can't stop myself from looking nervously at the stairs, the book trembling slightly in my hands.

Eventually, overwhelmed by exhaustion, I crawl into bed with Janis curled close beside me, leaving the light burning through the night.

I wake up and head downstairs for breakfast, where Mom has made pancakes and orange juice. Cherie joins us at the breakfast nook. The pancakes are really good—comforting, considering everything that happened yesterday. I'm still upset, but how can I even talk about it? Mom already thinks I'm seeing things that aren't there. It just makes me feel more isolated. I don't know what to do; I don't know how to make it go away.

"Would you like to go to the mall and shop for some school clothes?" Mom asks. Cherie and I both light up and immediately agree. This is just what I need. I leave the table and hurry upstairs to fix my hair, admiring my blue sundress and white sandals.

On the way to my room, I notice a portrait hanging crooked on the wall. It's in a part of the hallway I rarely walk through, near my parents' room. Curious, I step closer. It's a man with blond hair and dark bluish-green eyes, wearing a gray and white pinstripe suit. He's seated on a dark green Victorian couch beside a woman who looks strikingly similar to Beatrice. She's wearing a long white satin dress with a matching belt, covered by a black long-sleeved jacket, possibly felt, with a white fur collar. Black T-strap shoes complete the look.

If this is Beatrice, the man beside her isn't Arthur, my grandfather. In fact, he looks eerily like the guy from the store—the one who vanished. No, that's ridiculous. It's probably not Beatrice at all, just an old portrait from a well-known artist, which would explain why the family kept it. I scan the lower right-hand corner, looking for a signature, but there's something else. A tiny yellow piece of paper is tucked behind the frame. It looks like a note, but to retrieve it, I'd have to take the frame apart. I decide against it,

13

straighten the crooked portrait, and head back to my room to comb my hair.

Downstairs, I jump into the front seat next to Mom while Cherie climbs into the back. The mall isn't exactly close, but I don't mind—I love long drives. Mom tells us we can have lunch at the food court, which is a treat since we don't eat out very often. It also means we'll be there for a while.

When we arrive, Mom hands us each five dollars in the parking lot— pocket money in case we want to stop at the arcade or grab a pretzel. Excitement builds as we walk toward the entrance, but then I catch myself wondering if I'll see the blond man again. The thought sends a chill through me. I push it away.

The mall entrance is a series of glass doors set into a light gray stucco facade, with a large arch above reading *Paradise Shopping Mall.* What a misleading name. With a name like *Paradise,* it should be pink or some shade of purple, like a sunset—something more inviting.

Inside, we're assailed by bright lights and throngs of eager shoppers. Cherie and I head off to browse our favorite stores. The choices seem overwhelming as we peer through window after window. Eventually, I decide I like the new style of long shirts with leggings. I pick out a peach lace short-sleeve top and white knee-length leggings, along with a few other things. I can't wait to wear them. It's a wonderful day, my worries forgotten—at least for a while.

CHAPTER 4

*C*hatter swells through the elegant restaurant. The hum of refined voices mingles with the delicate clink of silverware against fine china, crisp white tablecloths draping over polished round tables, pink and dark pink chairs gleaming under the warm, diffused glow of ornate chandeliers. A sprawling mural of ocean waves crashing beneath a purplish-pink sunset stretches across the ceiling, its hues casting a dreamy light while fake palms sway gently in the corners, their fronds whispering a South Pacific breeze. A strikingly handsome blonde man, clad in a tailored dark blue pinstripe suit that mirrors the piercing depth of his ocean-blue eyes, extends a cigarette with a charming, almost mischievous smile. The young lady declines with a graceful, deliberate wave of her satin gloves, their lustrous sheen catching the chandelier's flicker. "I'm a nurse—it's bad for you," she says, her tone firm yet laced with a playful edge that dances in her voice like a melody.

He chuckles, a low, easy sound that rolls out warmly. "Everything is these days, Nora—life's just one long warning label." Her olive-green satin dress shimmers with intricate black sequins, their lace patterns swirling like midnight vines across the fabric. The sheer black cap sleeves flutter as she moves. A single red rose he presented her with earlier—a romantic gesture wrapped in old-world charm—rests beside her plate, its petals vibrant against the pristine white cloth. He reaches across the table, his hand brushing hers with tender intent as she lifts a pink-and-purple floral teacup to her lips, their smiles locking in a shared, unspoken warmth amid the symphony of clanking utensils and murmured conversations.

That night, I drift into a deep, contented sleep, my mind still buzzing from the joyous chaos of the mall trip with Mom and Cherie, their laughter echoing in my ears like a comforting lullaby. A sudden jolt rips me awake, a sensation of falling through endless dark, my stomach lurching as if I've tumbled off a cliff; then, just as quickly, I slip back into slumber, into a vivid dream. A majestic black horse races across our sprawling front yard, its mane whipping wildly in the wind, its hooves pounding the earth with frantic urgency. It rears up, a towering silhouette against the moonlit sky, as distant voices shout in alarm, their words muddled, while the low growl of a vehicle rumbles ominously from somewhere to my right. The horse bolts down the road, its gallop unfolding in eerie slow-motion, like a film reel stuttering through a projector, each frame lingering hauntingly before my eyes.

I wake again, my heart hammering in the pitch-black stillness of my room, the weight of the dream pressing on my chest; then, hours later, I stir to the soft glow of morning light filtering through my curtains, birds chirping a cheerful chorus outside. Dressing in a cozy pink long-sleeve shirt and matching leggings, I shuffle downstairs, my footsteps quiet on the hardwood. I hear faint whispers drifting from the library—soft, insistent murmurs that prickle my skin. I shrug them off, chalking it up to imagination, and head to the kitchen, pouring myself a bowl of cereal and a glass of orange juice.

A note on the fridge, scribbled in Mom's familiar scrawl, catches my eye: she's at the store helping Dad with errands, leaving Cherie in charge until she returns. I glance around—no sign of Cherie—so I savor my breakfast alone, the silence broken only by the crunch of cereal. Janis sniffs around the kitchen floor, her tiny paws tapping a rhythm; I scoop her up and step outside into the crisp morning air, the dew-kissed grass glinting under the sun. Cherie's out front, pedaling her bike in lazy circles with a friend, their giggles carrying on the breeze. She spots me and calls out, her voice sharp,

"Stay close to the house, okay?" I nod, cradling Janis, and wander toward the back trail, the forest path winding invitingly through the trees. Fifteen minutes in, my breath catches—the neighbor emerges from nowhere, silent as a shadow, no rustle of leaves to betray her approach. She's in her fifties, grey streaks threading through her tied-back hair, her slim, horse-rider frame taut, crankiness etched deep into her weathered face. Her sudden presence startles me, a chill racing down my spine as she looms there, uninvited.

She fixes me with a hard stare, her eyes narrowing for a long moment, then snaps in a clipped, authoritative tone, "Your mother's calling you—come with me now." The words ring hollow. Somehow, I'm certain she's lying, and without hesitation, I blurt out, "No, she's not—you're not telling the truth."

Janis barks sharply to my left, her small body tensing in my arms. I glance down at her, then back up—the neighbor's vanished, gone as abruptly as she appeared, leaving no trace on the leaf-strewn path. Janis yaps again, her gaze locked on a gnarled oak tree, but there's nothing—just the sway of branches in the wind. My chest coils tightly as I turn back toward home, the forest feeling heavier, the air thicker with something I can't name.

On the porch, I sink into a wrought iron chair, its cold metal biting through my leggings, guilt gnawing at me—helping the woman from my dream feels urgent, a desperate pull tugging at my heart, yet impossibly out of reach. I dismiss it with a shake of my head; I'm no psychic, no solver of ethereal mysteries. Cherie pedals by, her friend's chatter fading into the distance as I linger, lost in thought. I wander to the garden, drawn to a red rose bush bursting with blooms. Mom once told me it was Great-Grandmother's pride, its scarlet petals her favorite, a legacy rooted deep in our soil. The kitchen door bangs open—Mom's home, her arms laden with grocery bags, her face etched with fatigue as she announces plans for a late lunch, her voice weary but warm. I decide to grab my book from the library, my curiosity outweighing my unease as I climb the creaky back stairs, each step amplifying the silence.

I ease into the library, my eyes scanning the shadowed shelves lined with leather-bound volumes, the air thick with dust and quiet anticipation, and reach my worn recliner, its faded fabric cool against my hands as I settle in. A loud male voice booms out of nowhere, shattering the stillness like thunder: "How can she see us?" My breath catches, body freezing mid-motion as if turned to stone.

Another voice, calmer and measured, replies, "I don't know."

The first presses, urgent and sharp as a blade, "What is she?"

"I don't know," comes the steady, unflinching answer.

"We should kill her," the first declares, his tone cold and final, slicing through the air. I gasp, a sound trapped in my throat, heart slamming against my ribs with a frantic rhythm.

"NO REASON TO," the second counters, his voice unruffled, a steady anchor against the storm of the first; then a muffled word—"wife"—slips through, faint and fragmented, as if I'm hearing only pieces of a secret conversation veiled from me.

The second voice shifts, anger flaring like a sudden spark, "I'll take her."

Panic surges through me—I bolt for the stairs, legs trembling beneath me, but halfway down, I freeze, locked in place as if invisible hands are gripping my limbs, a scream for Mom tearing from my lungs, raw and desperate, echoing off the walls.

I call out to God, a frantic plea reverberating in my mind, my voice cracking with terror, and slowly, agonizingly, the unseen hold releases. I stumble down the remaining steps, tears streaming hot and unrelenting down my cheeks as Mom rushes up from the kitchen, her expression a mix of annoyance and reluctant concern.

"What's all this commotion about?" she demands, hands planted firmly on her hips, her apron streaked with flour. I breathlessly explain the voices, the chilling threat, my words tumbling over each other in a shaky rush. She sighs heavily, "It's just your imagination, honey—calm down, you're working yourself up over nothing."

I realize I forgot my book, abandoned in my terror on the recliner. I beg her to retrieve it, my voice small and pleading, and though grumbling about my dramatics, she reluctantly trudges upstairs. She returns with the book clutched in her hand, her skepticism validated. Janis barks at the kitchen stairs, her sharp and insistent yips piercing the air. I huddle at the breakfast nook, trying to steady my racing pulse with the book's familiar page. The morning's eerie weight lingers like a shadow that refuses to lift.

I ask Mom if I can go to the mall with Megan this week, my voice tentative, almost drowned by the lingering echo of my fear. She nods, a half-mocking smile tugging at her lips. "Good idea—get you out of this house for a bit, maybe shake off whatever's got you so jumpy."

I call Megan, relief washing over me like a cool wave when she agrees to go tomorrow, her mom offering to drive. Her cheerful tone is like a lifeline. That night, I sleep with the lamp on, its soft golden glow a fragile shield against the restless dark, shadows shifting uneasily across my walls like whispers made visible.

Morning creeps in slowly and heavily, the light dull through my window. I'm exhausted, dragging myself past the crooked portrait in the hall—that blond man with the striking bluish-green eyes, Beatrice in flowing white satin. I am wearing a purple shirt, floral shorts, and white sandals—Mom's favorite outfit, a small comfort—and I hurry to join her for breakfast: eggs scrambled golden, toast slathered with sweet blackberry jam, the kitchen warm and familiar.

Megan arrives, her white sundress shining against the muted porch light. Her mom trails behind, sending a cheerful wave that lifts my spirits. We pile into their car, chatting lightly as the town blurs past—shops with colorful awnings, people bustling along sidewalks, a fleeting glimpse of normalcy that soothes my frayed edges. Her mom asks about my summer, her voice kind and curious. I mumble, "reading, mostly." She nods, satisfied, the conversation fading into a comfortable quiet as we watch the world slip by.

We park at the mall, her mom lingering near the entrance as Megan and I dive into the arcade—air hockey pucks clatter across the table, skee-ball machines whir with triumphant beeps and flashes. Megan's on a streak, racking up tickets with a gleeful grin, trading them for a stash of Nerds and tart lemon candy, splitting the haul with me as we wander the bustling halls, our laughter cutting through the din of shoppers and distant music.

Megan's mom treats us to warm pretzels before we head out, salt clinging to my fingers as I tear off bites. She invites me to swim Friday, and

I grin, the thought of escape bittersweet—I dread going home, to the strangeness waiting there like an uninvited guest lurking in the corners.

Back home, Mom greets us with a tired but genuine smile, her mood visibly improved from the morning's strain. Megan and her mom leave after a quick, friendly chat at the door, the soft thud of it closing echoing in the now-quiet house like a sigh of relief. I change into old clothes—worn jeans and a faded tee—and join Cherie in the garden, sunglasses shielding my eyes from the relentless sun, my straw hat floppy from past beach days, its brim casting a jagged shadow. We pull weeds in silence, the sun beating down on our backs, until a thunderous gallop shakes the air—a black horse charges down the asphalt road in front of our house, rearing wildly with a fierce grace. It's just like my dream, its mane a dark storm whipping against the daylight.

The neighbor's voice cuts through, shrill and commanding: "Midnight!" She's leaning out her truck window, husband beside her gripping the wheel, chasing the beast as it bolts in that same slow-motion reel, dust swirling in its wake like a ghostly trail. I turn to Mom, my voice small and hesitant. "Were you calling me yesterday?"

She frowns, puzzled, her brow furrowing. "No, you knew I was at the store—why do you ask?" Her eyes narrow with a mix of concern and exasperation. "You're acting strange lately, you know that?"

Her words sting, a sharp blend of truth and dismissal. I'm stunned but not surprised. She can't grasp what's unraveling around me. I barely understand it myself. The neighbor trudges back down the road, leading Midnight by the reins with a weary slump, her husband's truck rumbling slowly behind, its engine a low growl.

Tony pedals up on his bike, waving and flashing that wide, easy grin that lights up his face. He hops off to join us, tugging weeds with a fervor that matches his wild, animated tales—stories of the horse's dramatic escape, of rodeos he dreams of riding in one day, his voice bright and brimming with excitement, painting vivid pictures of lassoed stallions and cheering crowds. Mom brings out lemonade, tart and cool in sweating glasses, the ice clinking as we sit in the garden.

Dusk creeps in slowly, softening the edges of the day, Tony's chatter weaving a warm thread through the fading light, his enthusiasm infectious.

Mom invites him over for lasagna, her tone softening with a rare warmth. He calls home, gets the okay from his mom, and agrees to stay, settling at our table with a grin. We eat early so Tony can make it home before dark. Cherie picks at her food, quiet and withdrawn, but Mom's laughter rings out at Tony's heartfelt compliments, her mood thawing as he devours seconds, praising her cooking with boyish delight. The kitchen glows with the comfort of shared stories. When dinner's over, he bikes off under a starry sky. I can't help but smile. Despite its eerie, unsettling start, the day ends wonderfully, wrapped in the unexpected comfort of friendship and family.

CHAPTER 5

$\mathcal{N}$ora scribbles notes on her patient's progress, clipboard steady in her hands. Another nurse beckons her to the front desk, shattering her focus—a jolt she veils with a tight smile, hazel eyes glinting with strain. She glances at her patient, a fragile shape in a white metal bed, breath a faint thread in the sterile hush. Nora clips the board in place above the bed and strides off.

At the desk, she's met with the scent of white lilies and red roses, a quiet defiance against the ward's harsh antiseptic background. She reads the card: *To my darling Nora, with love, Rodney.* A flush warms her cheeks as she grabs the bouquet and stows it gently in her locker, a secret prize waiting for later.

I sift through my jewelry box, searching for my lost amethyst ring. It's not there. I yank open my dresser, six drawers groaning, my fingers probing edges where it might've slipped. No, just clothes. In my closet, shirts sway silently beside shoes, but I swear I hear something, a whisper snaking through the dark—air seeping from behind. The drywall's thin, cold, alive; a shiver claws up my spine.

Janis bounds in, tail wagging, begging for a scratch. I pet her, but her gaze fixes on the closet, and she lets out a low rumbling growl. I slam the door and head downstairs. Halfway down, I hear a man's voice murmuring my name, slow and thick with intent. I spin around, my heart hammering, but all I see is empty steps. Janis, cradled close, turns with me. "Hear that?" I whisper, but she leaves my dread unanswered.

In the kitchen, I set Janis down, nerves fraying in the stillness. No one's here. She senses my panic, and her calm offers a thin lifeline. The phone rings. It's Megan, her voice slicing through the heavy silence. We chat, then I hang up to fetch the mail. Dusk is already painting the sky in muted streaks.

Outside, a wolf stands across the road from the mailbox, its blue-green eyes piercing me like icy daggers. Janis safe inside, I snatch the mail and back off, tentatively and fearfully. It holds still, watching me, unmoving. When I reach the porch, I dart inside and fumble the lock shut, my mind wrestling shadows.

I rush upstairs where I find Cherie in the library, her presence a soft ward. Somehow the weirdness fades with others near. I sink into my recliner, thoughts spinning, Janis curled at my feet. Mom calls us down for a dinner of fried chicken, mashed potatoes, corn, biscuits. I savor each bite, grounding myself in the simple pleasure.

After dinner, I follow Cherie back to the library, a haven. By nine, she heads to bed. I take the cue and head to my room, too, the thought of solitude unbearable. Janis is gone, and her absence gnaws at me as I drift into restless sleep.

I wake, darkness pressing like a shroud, half-aware. I sense a man to the right of me, looming, unshakable. In a dark voice he urges me to leave with him. "No," I snap, dread surging. "Who are you?"

"The man from the grocery store," he says, his words like a twisted hook.

"What do you want?"

"Marry me."

"What? I'm just a child!" I can't believe what I'm hearing. "Don't you have a wife?"

His voice sinks low. He tells me his wife's dead. He blurts out that he's rich but quickly seems to regret it, like it's something he shouldn't have said. Something about his tone sparks pity despite my confusion. He says I was flirting with him in the store, warping it into this mad proposal. "Pack," he demands, his urgency rising.

I'm rooted in fear. I nod into the void, trying to stall him. He's pleased and presses me again. I freeze, unable to breathe. He seems to understand my hesitation. "I'll return when you're forty," he says softly.

"But why would you want someone so old?"

"Don't worry, I can reverse your age."

"How?" I demand, trembling. Silence. "Stay single—you'll only have my children," he snarls. He reaches out and touches my left ovary, his hand searing with cold fire. I see a contract in my mind—a marriage contract. Without thinking I scrawl an X. I see different kinds of rings, and I choose an antique silver one. Pleased, the man turns to leave.

"Wait," I call out, "what's your name?"

He says something, but it's hard to understand. "Just call me Niffin," he says, laughing, glee prickling with power.

"I'm twelve," I whisper, lost. "What's a niffin?"

He stares at me for a moment silently before beginning to move away. "I'll be back for you when you turn forty." I feel his kiss icy—is it real? I jolt awake. I'm sure that was no dream, and a sense of doom washes over me.

The lamp's frail glow steadies me. Janis is barking downstairs, frantic, piercing the night until Dad checks on her and calms her down. I fade out, waking groggily to sunlight and birds. Downstairs, I raid the leftovers, helping myself to a drumstick, thigh, potatoes, and lemonade. I notice that Janis is missing. Where is she?

Mom looks me over and says, "Rough night?"

"You don't know the half of it," I mutter heavily.

"Megan's pool today," she says. I'd forgotten all about it, Niffin clogging my mind. Trying to establish some sense of normalcy, I put on my navy swimsuit, purple-white shirt, pink leggings, and sandals, seeking familiar comfort against the dark.

As we arrive at Megan's, I turn to Mom, uncertain how to put my feelings into words. I stare at her momentarily and then ask, "Have you seen anything strange lately?"

She pauses for a moment before replying. "We're always here to talk if you need it."

We roll into Megan's gray-brick driveway. Mom is clearly impressed by the landscaping. I ring the bell. Heavy wood doors, grey with floral carvings, swing wide. Megan's voice rings out in greeting as she welcomes us inside.

Her house is sprawling—spiral stairs, a huge living room, the kitchen gleaming with tan cabinets and green tile. She hands me lemonade, tart and bright. Mom sorts out the plans and then leaves to help Dad.

We hit the pool, a playful game of Marco Polo helping splash all my tension away. Megan's mom brings Rice Krispies treats and lemonade, perfect and crisp in the heat. Megan's excited to be starting school and asks if I want to take riding lessons with her. I nod, picturing flowing manes and boots and braids. Megan's mom returns with ham and cheese sandwiches and chips. We enjoy our lunch on the lanai, lounging in the purple patio chairs.

Mom picks me up near dinner time. I linger reluctantly, but it's been hours. I wave goodbye to Megan and her mom as we head out to the car.

After dinner, I join Cherie in the library, her quiet presence a bulwark. I read until exhaustion starts to overwhelm me. I say goodnight to my sister, who seems annoyed by the distraction.

Sleep brings a vivid tropical dream, filled with warm sun and pleasant voices, but then the scene suddenly shifts. There's a man stalking me, chasing me through the resort. I see the scene from far away, watching it unfold as he pursues me relentlessly. I wake with a start, my heart pounding in the dark. It feels too real. I flick the lamp on and go to grab some water. I feel so parched. Janis is napping by the kitchen door. I wonder if she'd be a good guard against Niffin. But she's sleeping peacefully, and I don't want to bother her. Maybe tomorrow. I head back upstairs and collapse into my bed. I ache for normal, the life I had before Niffin.

CHAPTER 6

The room swells with loud jazz music, the live band pouring sound into every corner. Nora pauses, her eyes catching the saxophone player, curiosity tugging at her for a fleeting second. Rodney's hand finds hers, warm and sure, pulling her toward the dance floor. She meets his gaze, her large custom ring with its glass blue stone flashing as they slip into the fox trot. The dance hall thrums with eager, friendly faces—people here for the jazz, for the ballroom dances, for the night itself. Nora's long teal satin cocoon gown flows around her, loose and light, cinched at the waist by a silver belt buckle. Her black T-strap heels tap the floor, and her hair sits high in a bun, a teal jeweled hairband circling it, peacock feathers clustering to the right like a quiet boast.

Murals climb the walls, bold and bright, one sprawling across the ceiling where a grand chandelier dangles, spilling light. The band plays on a stage, dark green velvet curtains framing them, and the music's vibration hums through the floor, alive underfoot as the crowd dances. It's a lovely scene, warm and loud, and Nora knows it'll stick with her. It's one of those nights she'll carry forever, sharp and sweet in her memory.

I stop at the library stairs, a knot tightening in my chest. Is Cherie up there? I call her name, voice wobbling in the second-floor hallway. "Yeah," she answers, soft but clear, pulling me up.

I climb and drop into my recliner, the blue fabric cool against my skin. Her eyes narrow, and after a moment she says, "You've been clingy lately—like you hate being alone."

I scoff, brushing it off. "You're exaggerating."

Her head tilts, a smirk growing. "Afraid of ghosts?"

"Why? Have you seen any?" I ask, serious now, my voice low.

She blinks, caught off guard, then leans in. "Wait, seriously? Are you actually scared of ghosts?"

I force a shaky laugh. "No, they're not real. You're being silly." But the words feel hollow—recent shadows make them hard to believe. I'm not sure if I'm trying to fool her or myself.

Later, Mom takes us to the grocery store, the car humming under the heavy sun. Fireworks gleam from displays—Fourth of July stacks of red, white, and blue. "Can we throw a party for the neighborhood kids?" I ask with shining eyes. "Maybe have Megan over too?"

Mom nods, a small smile breaking her stern edges, and I grab packages—sparklers, bang snaps, little bursts of joy. She also agrees red, white, and blue cupcakes and matching Kool-Aid. I'm buzzing, already picturing the neighborhood kids and especially Megan's happy smile.

"Can Megan sleep over that night?" I push.

"If her mom says yes, sure," she says softly. It's a maybe, but it's enough.

Back home, I rush to the phone, dialing Megan fast. "Party at my place for the Fourth—sleepover, too, if you can!" She laughs, promising to check with her mom and call back. Her happy voice lingers in my ear as I hang up.

I bolt down the street, sneakers slapping the pavement, knocking on doors. Tony's first. "Yeah, I'm in!" he says eagerly. A few other kids nod, too, and then Leslie, the new girl, agrees with a shy dip of her head. Her dark hair swings and I feel a little thrill of victory.

Mom's voice drifts from the kitchen when I get back. "We'll need a festive tablecloth—plates, cups, napkins too." She's in it with me now, tossing out ideas. "Maybe sugar cookies with red and blue sprinkles." I can hear the growing excitement in her tone as she turns to Cherie. "You inviting your friends?"

Cherie rattles off the names of neighborhood kids and school friends. My party's stretching, spilling over, and I feel a twinge—like it's not mine anymore. But it's bigger now, better, and I can't argue with that.

Another thought hits me, quiet but firm. "Can we start going back to church?" I ask Mom. She looks at me, surprised, then smiles—a real one. "I'll think about it."

My pink Bible sits on my dresser, unopened, because I never look at it outside Sunday school. But Niffin's shadow lingers in my head, pushing me toward faith, toward something solid.

A week rolls by, quiet and steady—no Niffin, no prickling stares. I can almost forget it all, like maybe it wasn't real. The party's today, and Megan's mom said yes to the sleepover. I'm feeling lighter and happy again. Mom's in the kitchen, vanilla cupcakes cooling, half slathered in red frosting, half in blue. Festive stripes of color line the counter.

Cherie and I tackle the Kool-Aid. I rip open cherry red packets, the powder staining my fingers, while she stirs blueberry, the pitcher swirling purple. Mom's sugar cookies smell heavenly, their golden edges peeking out, and we wait to dust them with red and blue sprinkles. "Let's do the cupcakes, too," I say, grinning. "Blue on red, red on blue." Cherie nods, flashing a rare smile, and we scatter sprinkles, laughing as they stick to our hands.

Mom hauls out two tablecloths—red, white, and blue stripes—draping them over the wrought-iron tables on the porch. The first, by the entrance, holds cupcakes on a big blue plate and cookies on a red one. The second's got Kool-Aid in plastic pitchers—also red and blue—flanked by matching cups. Plates and napkins with fireworks bursting on them are stacked high the first table, loud against the quiet dusk.

Night falls, and the guests start to trickle in. Mom flips on the porch light, a warm glow spilling out into the night. Megan's mom drops her off, a tray of ham and cheese sandwiches and a bag of chips in her hands. She steps up from the kitchen, smiling wide.

Tony's the next to arrive, fireworks tucked under his arm, his grin sharp. And there's Leslie, quiet and alone. Cherie's friends pile in, too, loud and laughing. Tony's eyes keep finding me, cutting through the chatter, following me in every conversation. Megan sees what's happening and smirks over her sandwich.

The night builds to a frenzy. Sparklers flare, and we wave them with abandon, circles and zigzagging light streaking through the darkness. Tony lights his stash. A tank spins, spitting sparks, bold and wild. The food sits forgotten until Mom calls from the porch, "Come eat!"

She and Dad are perched there, watching us, smiles on their faces. It feels good—no eerie weight, no unseen eyes. Normal's creeping back, soft and sure. I've half-forgotten the weirdness, with thoughts of school hinting at a fresh start. Relief washes over me, warm as the night air.

Mom flips on the radio, turning to a popular station. We dive into the cupcakes, cookies, and sandwiches, smoke from fireworks curling all around us. My parents' laughter drifts from the porch, easy and light. Tony and Megan stick close to me, their voices cutting through the din.

We cluster by the porch, light pooling around us. As the fireworks start to fizzle out, Megan breaks into the electric slide, her steps clumsy but sure. Tony has a harder time, tripping with a grin, his eyes again flicking toward me.

A car rolls up; it's Leslie's dad. "Night!" we call out as she grabs a red-frosted cupcake. She thanks us in a soft voice and heads out. Tony's mom pulls in next. He frowns, dragging his feet, but perks up when Mom offers leftovers. He snags a sandwich and a few cookies, and I catch myself smiling at him.

One by one, the kids peel off, until it's just Megan and me, the radio buzzing low in the background. She says she has her sights set on cheerleading next year. "I'm taking lessons," she says brightly.

"Horseback riding still?" I ask, my voice tight.

"Yeah, sure," she says, but she seems less interested, distracted. She's never cared about cheerleading before—why now?

I feel a twinge. Could it be a betrayal? Maybe, but it's too soon to put a name on it. "What's with cheerleading?" I press.

She grins and casually replies. "The neighborhood girls are doing it. Mom thinks it's fun, a sport." I blink. Those girls are popular and rich. That's not *us*. Our friendship's odd to some, I know because I'm not part of that crowd. But I'm liked enough, well, at least by Megan.

Mom calls time for bed. "Megan's bag's in your room," she says, "and a sleeping bag for you. She gets the bed."

I click off the radio, and Cherie and I start to clean up while Megan hauls the leftovers inside. Mom packs them in Tupperware, the pitchers sloshing into the fridge. Megan sneaks a sugar cookie, grinning as we head up to my room. I push my door open. Her bag's by the closet, and there's a sleeping bag near the nightstand. I untie it, spread it out, and grab my pillow. Mom slips in with a guest pillow for Megan. "Sheets are fresh," she says proudly.

We settle in, talking, doodling in my "dork book." It's my sketchpad, filled with drawings of the Planters Peanut guy, with Ms. Almond, his girl-friend, and his arch-nemesis. Silly, I know, but it's mine. The stories make me laugh. My drawing's are rough, but Megan's are so much better. Her sketches are smooth and sure, and I have to suppress a tiny bit of jealousy. "Let's make a comic," I say. "I write, you draw." She nods, and we sketch some more. If I'm being honest, our horse is a little lopsided—but it's ours.

Janis pads in, and we pet her, forgetting the dork book. "Tony was staring all night," Megan teases. I blush and stammer denials, but she's not having it. In truth, I'm secretly thrilled because I definitely like him back.

Eventually, sleep pulls us under. The sleeping bag's stiff, but it's only one night. I drift off, Mr. Peanut galloping through my head in a new wild tale. I'll tell Megan about it tomorrow.

Sunlight wakes us. I stretch, feeling Janis curled tight against me. I slip out of the room, letting Megan dress, and head down to the kitchen. I look around and grab a sugar cookie before breakfast. Cherie's there, too, snag-ging a blue cupcake, and we share a conspiratorial glance. Mom's steps echo from the living room, and we bolt upstairs, Tupperware clattering, laughter chasing us.

Megan's in a pink shirt and jean shorts, with her hair in a ponytail. I duck inside the room, swapping my clothes for a purple shirt and floral shorts. I wish I had my amethyst and wonder where it could have gone while brushing my hair.

Downstairs, Mom's at the nook, pancakes are sizzling, and orange juice poured. We eat, chatter filling the air. The phone rings. Cherie grabs it, says

"Hello?" twice, then slams it down. "They didn't say anything," she says frowning, "just hung up."

"Weird," says Mom.

Megan's mom shows up a little after breakfast. After she's gone, Mom asks how the sleepover went. "Megan's into cheerleading now," I say, flatly.

"She just growing up, trying new things," Mom replies, brushing it off.

Sunday, we attend church. Mom's in a tan skirt, pink blouse, pink heels. Cherie's white dress blooms with pinkish-purple flowers, her sandals clicking a wholesome accompaniment. I've got on a light blue sundress and tan sandals. Dad's gray suit is set off nicely by a purple shirt.

The brick church looms ahead, white double doors hanging open and steps climbing to an open porch. A table and mirror sit in the entry, with flyers scattered around. Mom strides down the pink carpet, picking up the back pew. We sit down together, the wood creaking under our weight. The choir's set up front in neat white chairs, and the pulpit's adorned with artificial flowers. The high ceiling features eight gold chandeliers and five arched windows on each side with floral designs.

People nod in greeting, welcoming us back, saying they hope we're going to stay. The service starts like I remember: announcements, choir, the message. When it's over, Dad suggests lunch—a rare treat. Mom picks a spot near the church, and we go. It's a cheeseburger for me, salad for Mom, and chicken fingers for Cherie and Dad.

Once we get home, I change out of my church clothes, set my Bible on the dresser, and promise myself I'll read it daily. I'll pray, too. It's time to let new roots grow.

I take Janis out on the trail for a hike. It's a sunny day, with birds chirping happily in the light breeze. A thought suddenly strikes me, and I stop and pray for a horse. *Please, God, a horse named Blessing.* Janis bounds around me as the words pour out.

When we get back to the house, I read my Bible a bit, then doodle. Of course I draw Mr. Peanut on horseback, clumsy but mine. When sleep calls, I crawl into bed, Janis close by. It's a habit now, and I relish her steady warmth.

In the morning, it's breakfast, then a bike ride. I'm hoping to see Tony, but he's not out. I do spot Leslie in her yard, waving at me. I stop, and we chat for a while, her voice soft against the breeze.

When I get back home, I call Megan and ask if we can do something, but she's hanging out with friends from her neighborhood today. I try to hide my disappointment. "Mall soon?" I ask.

"How about Friday?" she asks.

"I'll ask Mom," I tell her, hanging up.

Mom's in the garden. "Horseback lessons?" I ask. She nods, promising to find a place. Things are starting to feel right. I decide to read my Bible and pray—especially for a horse named Blessing.

CHAPTER 7

*N*ora clutches her new blue cloche hat tight, a gift from Rodney, to keep the wind from pulling it away while they drive. The convertible's roof is down, allowing the sun to pour over them on this bright day. She notices the wooden steering wheel, long and sturdy, attached to a metal rod with three silver pedals beneath it. The left one makes the car go, the middle one reverses it, and the right one brings it to a stop. They look more like gears than anything else, she thinks.

There's not much to look at in Rodney's Ford Model T. The spartan black interior contrasts with the wooden wheel, and a few gauges and levers dot the dashboard, simple and plain. Nora doesn't own a car yet, but now that she works as a nurse at the hospital, she plans to save for one. She loves the idea of freedom a car brings, the chance to go anywhere whenever she pleases. This Saturday drive was Rodney's idea, and she quickly agreed, packing a picnic basket with sandwiches and fruit for a lunch stop along the way.

I sit at the kitchen nook and pick up the phone to call Megan so I can ask her about going to the mall. I hope she still wants to go with me. I dial her number with nervous anxiety, especially when I hear Megan answer the phone.

"Oh, I forgot to ask Mom about it," Megan replies casually. "I'll call you back later."

I hang up, confused and hurt by her nonchalance. This isn't the Megan I know, my friend, the sweetest girl in our class. That girl always cared. I stay there for a moment, staring at the table, before getting up to grab a drink from the refrigerator. The cold glass in my hand doesn't shake the feeling, so I decide to go outside and try to distract myself.

I grab my bike from the porch, the screen door banging shut behind me, and start riding down the road, hoping to run into some of my friends. The fresh air is a welcome relief, brushing my face as I pedal. I ride past Tony's house and notice his mom's car isn't in the driveway, so he's probably not home. I keep going and spot Leslie in her front yard, circling on her bike. I stop and say hi. She starts talking about her summer—swimming, reading, small things—and I listen, even though it feels a bit dull. With no one else around, I'm happy for the company, so I just nod along. She suggests we take the trail through the woods down the road.

Kids use that path often. It's a winding dirt track that cuts through the trees and pops out in another neighborhood. Leslie leads the way, and as we ride, she points out an abandoned treehouse. Eyeing the rickety frame and the roof half-caved from a fallen branch, I ask if it's safe to go up there. "It's fine," she insists. "I've been up there plenty of times." She starts climbing the wooden strips nailed to the trunk. I follow, but unease starts prickling at me.

We step inside the treehouse. Well, it's really just a small, rustic space with leaves—new and old—scattered across the floor. I don't see the appeal, but Leslie says it's the hot spot for neighborhood kids, who argue over who gets it and when. Shrugging she says, "It's free right now!" I stand there unsure, listing to the wind whistling through hundreds of gaps. "Sometimes we bring board games or cards up here to play," she tells me.

The wind picks up, howling through the treehouse, and the old plywood floor creaks under my feet as I shift. I can't help worrying about it collapsing and me falling through. "Are you sure this is safe? This floor feels like it could go at any minute."

Leslie gives me a little smirk, as if I'm some overcautious mom. I feel silly but still on edge. After a while, Leslie's brother climbs up to join us, the boards groaning under his weight. I've never met him before, and he doesn't seem friendly. He has a smug demeanor that makes it seem like he doesn't like me much. I can feel it in the way he barely glances my way. I tell myself I'm branching out and making new friends, and this is just a new experience. Yeah, I doubt I'll bother with him again, but Leslie seems okay.

We head back after a bit, riding our bikes together and talking about the upcoming start of school. It's her first year at my school, and she admits she's nervous about making friends. "It'll be fine," I assure her. "Most of the kids there are nice enough."

"Would you like to come over to my house sometime soon?" she asks.

"Sure," I respond quickly. "But it's getting kind of late, and I need to get home for dinner." I peel off toward my house, feeling more alone as I ride, missing Megan and hoping she calls.

When I get home, I check the refrigerator for any notes about Megan calling. There's nothing, so I grab another glass of lemonade and head upstairs to my room. Depression creeps in out of nowhere, heavy and thick. I wonder how much of it ties to Megan or if it's something else. I try to read my Bible and pray that evening, but my mind drifts to my irregular periods. I've had a few, but they're never consistent. I wonder if it's connected to Niffin touching my ovary that night, a thought that chills me.

I fall asleep eventually, but a nightmare jolts me awake. A man with a knife is chasing me through the mall, past the fountain, my feet pounding against the tile. I hide in the arcade, my heart slamming, terror gripping me until he leaves. It feels too real, too vivid. I wake up sweating. The room's still dark, and I pull off my top blanket to cool down. Sleep takes me again, dreamless this time.

Morning comes, and I wake up groggy, thinking about what to wear. But I notice a strange bruise on my forearm—three marks, like a handprint. I wonder if it's from the dream, but that's impossible. He never touched me in it, but the bruise wasn't there when I went to bed. It's sore and swollen, and I know it'll darken soon. I shake my head, confused.

I decide to give Megan a few more days to call about the mall. If she doesn't, I guess I'll just ask Leslie or another girl instead. The depression from yesterday lingers, and I hope seeing Leslie today might lift it. I pick out a purple long-sleeve shirt, thin enough for summer but good for covering the bruise—something I'd wear to a cold restaurant or theater. Downstairs, Mom's making breakfast—the usual eggs, toast, and orange juice. She notices the shirt and asks if I'm cold. "I'm not feeling great," I say, "and I'm a little chilly." She looks concerned but doesn't say anything, handing me my food instead.

After breakfast, I bike to Leslie's house. She's walking down the street with her brother. "Want to join me for a ride" I ask.

"Yes!" she exclaims. She grabs her bike, and slings a shopping bag with board games over the handlebars. We head out together, the bag swinging as she pedals.

We reach the treehouse, and Tony's bike is parked there, along with a few of his friends' bikes. I feel a lift in my chest and call up to him. He pokes his head out the door. "Hi," he calls, "Who's that with you?"

I introduce Leslie, climbing the steps while she hangs back. I ask if we can join them with the games. I can hear his friends groan in the background, obviously not thrilled, but Tony invites us up to see what we've brought and if they're interested.

Leslie unpacks Monopoly and Operation from her bag. Tony and his friends settle on Operation, and we start playing. Everyone laughs when the buzzer goes off, Tony seeming like the steadiest at first but then trailing off. Something's not right, though. He's not talking to me much, or Leslie either, and I feel a cold distance from him that wasn't there before.

After a while I check my watch—it's lunchtime. "I'm gonna head home for a sandwich. Maybe I'll come back after if you're still here."

I climb down, glancing at Tony as I go, but he doesn't look up from the game. What's happening? Both Megan and Tony, two people I was close to, acting weird. I bike home alone in my thoughts.

Mom's in the kitchen when I walk in. "Would you like a peanut butter and jelly sandwich?" she asks.

"Yes," I say, "with milk." I pull the peanut butter, grape jam, and milk from the fridge. She joins me at the table and asks how my day's going. "It's okay. I've been with Leslie."

She notices my hands and looks up questioningly. "Why aren't you wearing your amethyst ring?"

I hesitate and admit I misplaced it. She seems disappointed but offers to help me look for it later and keep an eye out around the house. I thank her and smile. She pauses, lost in thought, then smiles faintly. "What are you thinking about?" I ask.

"I had this dream a long time ago," she begins. "A man broke into a woman's house and stole her jewelry. He cut himself escaping through a window, hid the goods, and then bled to death."

I freeze. "I— I had the same dream not long ago, the exact same dream!" Mom shrugs, like it's no big deal. How can she be so calm? I don't mention my bruise or last night's nightmare. I'm confused and don't know if I can trust her.

I go upstairs to read my Bible and pray for a bit. Janis slips into my room. It's been too long since I spent time with her. I'm getting too wrapped up in all this. If Megan and Tony are pulling away, that's on them. I haven't done anything to push them off.

I head back to the treehouse. Leslie's the only one still there. She says she went home for lunch too. I'm disappointed Tony's gone, but there's nothing I can do about it. "What does your brother think of me?" I ask

She smiles and says, "He thinks you're a dork." I'm taken aback, a little offended even—he's not exactly cool himself.

The board games are still up there, and Leslie asks if I still want to play. I agree to Operation again, though I'm tired of it. We climb up and start to play. Leslie talks a lot—about her parents' beliefs and religion. "What do you think about God?"

"He's my savior," I reply quickly.

"We're all gods," she says with a smirk, "and we reach it through illu-mination."

"That's blasphemy!"

Leslie just shrugs and says she and her mom talk about New Age stuff all the time, especially in the car. They both seem so odd, and I don't know what to say.

We finish up after a while. Leslie packs up her games, and we ride back together. I say goodbye and head home. On the way, I pass Tony and his friends. One of them looks at me and says to Tony, "She's ugly," loud enough for me to hear. Tony flinches—he knows I caught it. I pedal faster, that guy's smirk burning behind me, and keep going.

Depression grows heavier as I ride. Life should be better with all the Bible reading and prayer. It's not.

I decide to go to bed early, taking Janis with me. Megan hasn't called all day, and my mood sinks further. I climb into bed and try to sleep, but I just lie there in my thoughts. Suddenly, I hear my doorknob turn and shut. I look up fast—no one's there, no sound. Darkness presses in, and I black out, waking to the morning light.

When I get up, I check for new bruises—nothing today. Janis follows me downstairs to the kitchen. Mom comes in from the living room and says we're going to the grocery store. I'm surprised that I actually look forward to it, just to get out. In the car, I think about last night—the doorknob, the blackout. I hope it's just my imagination.

At the store, Mom skips a cart, saying we don't need to get much. After grabbing a few things, she changes her mind and points to an abandoned cart down an aisle, asking me to get it. I wheel it back, and a lady storms up, yelling that it's hers, that I'm stealing it. I'm shocked. She's furious, and I don't even know if it was hers. Mom steps in. "Sorry," she says. "We thought it was free." The lady grabs it and stalks off. I've never had someone snap at me like that.

Back home, Tony's lingering outside. I help Mom with the groceries, then go over to see him.

"Hey, I'm sorry for my friend." He looks genuinely sorry.

"It's okay."

"I, um, I think I met the right girl," he says a little sheepishly. "Do you think I should tell her?"

I assume he means me and smile, giggling, "Oh yes, you should."

We talk more until his friends ride up, calling him to join them at Mike's house. He says goodbye and leaves. Hope flickers inside. Maybe Tony's still the same with me, and good news is coming.

Just then Mom steps out. "Phone for you. It's Megan."

I rush inside, my heart leaping. Megan says we can go to the mall Friday. I hang up, joy rushing back. Maybe things are normal again.

That evening, I go to the library to read alone. I'm feeling confident that whatever has been happening, it's all settling down. Janis curls up at my feet as I turn pages for hours. There are no whispers, no eerie calls, just like old times. I head to bed, drifting off thinking about Friday with Megan, my best friend. But as sleep takes me, the doorknob turns, opens, and shuts. I flick on the lamp—nothing there. I turn it off, listening hard, feeling watched, a presence heavy in the room. Then I black out. I wake in the morning, rattled. Prayer and Bible aren't helping. Maybe I'll stop for a while and see if life gets better without them.

CHAPTER 8

*N*ora steps out of the church and looks down at her black T-strap shoes, noticing the worn edges. She hopes she still looks nice, but her nurse's income is modest, and new shoes aren't within reach yet. Rodney waits for her, leaning against a post with an easy smile. He falls into step beside her, carefree, with no plan—just happy to be there. She smiles back and suggests a restaurant for hot tea and pastries.

The waitress brings their tea in elegant cups, delicate blue floral patterns circling them, set on matching saucers. They sit at a small table with a crisp white cloth and two wooden chairs by a large window. Outside, the street bustles with people walking, cars rolling, horse buggies clopping along, and the occasional dog or cat darting by.

I sit at the breakfast nook with my cereal spoon in my hand, my mind spinning, thinking about how to fix everything. Mom walks in, her voice bright with good news. I ask what it is, half-hoping it's about my hidden troubles. "I've found a place for horseback riding lessons. You start next week."

I can hardly contain my excitement. Well, at least one thing's going right. But there's still that weirdness. I stir my spoon and ask Mom a hypothetical question. "What would you think if something kept opening and closing your door, but you couldn't see anything?"

She pauses, looking at me, then answers seriously. "Could be aliens." I stare at her, and she continues, "I've noticed weird stuff too—like those footprints on the railing, when you said something grabbed your ankle. I've seen them before." She explains that a few weeks before that day, she'd been in the kitchen checking dinner, stepped out into the garden, and found footprints on the porch railing. "You were biking, Cherie was down the street—no one was home. I've heard whispers from the library, too, and I understand why you're scared to go up there."

"How could it be aliens? Why?" Mom just shrugs, and the conversation drops.

My depression is deepening into discouragement. I'm losing the desire to read the Bible, pray, or even engage in my hobbies. I feel stuck, stagnant, like the past few months have frozen me in place. I decide to go for a bike ride, hoping Leslie's around to fill the day. Tomorrow's the mall day with Megan, so at least I have something to hold onto.

I pedal down the road toward Leslie's house, the wind sharp against my face. In the distance, I see Tony and Leslie together, hurrying toward her place. He's holding a board game, urging her to move faster. My stomach sinks—*that's* what he meant. Tony and Leslie are a pair now. It was her he was talking about, not me. They don't notice me watching, and that cuts just as deep. I turn away and ride home, unable to look anymore.

When I get back, Mom's in the kitchen. She can see my expression and asks what's wrong. I tell her about Tony and Leslie. Her response is blunt. "He told you he liked someone else."

"But I thought it was me."

She looks puzzled. "Well, I don't know how you got that idea."

I'm too sad to argue. Instead, I head to the library to read, Janis padding after me and curling at my feet. The sinking feeling is growing. It's my first real heartbreak, and I wish Mom had offered more than cold logic.

That night, I drift off to sleep, but it's strange. I feel awake yet not awake. I'm standing in the street outside my house. Above me, spaceships are hovering. There's a triangle, a square, a circle, a rectangle, all made of crys-

41

tal, transparent with an iridescent shine as they glide past. A man's voice speaks. "Where did you go?"

"I'm here," I reply.

"Are you okay? Do you need anything?"

"No, I'm fine," I lie.

"I love you," he says, soft and clear. I wake up with a start, sadness and loneliness washing over me. Time felt still in that dream, and I have no idea what it is I'm longing for.

I try to go back to sleep, but I can't stop thinking about the dream, a quiet ache growing. Somehow, I drift off, and when morning comes, I head downstairs. Mom's making tea. "Megan's picking you up later to go to the mall." I feel a flicker of happiness, but the dream is still haunting me.

"Tell me about Leslie and the neighborhood kids," Mom says. "What do you do for fun?" I'm not sure why she's asking. I mean, it's just normal neighborhood stuff. I tell her about the treehouse, biking, and the trail to the other side. Then, for some crazy reason, I lie and say there's an old, abandoned horse stable near the treehouse. I don't know why I say it. There's some sharp, sudden pressure pushing me to lie, growing stronger until I give in. It stops the moment I speak, and I recognize it—telepathic, like Niffin's energy, testing me. I should've fought harder. I don't tell Mom it's a lie. I don't know if she'd understand or believe me about that force.

The phone breaks the silence. I answer, saying hello repeatedly. No one responds, and after a minute, I hang up. "Megan will be here soon," Mom says. "You'd better go get ready."

I head upstairs and pick out a long white shirt, pink leggings, and white sandals, then wait in the living room, watching the clock tick slowly. Megan and her mom pull up, and I run to the door to greet them. Our moms talk for a minute or two, and then we leave for the mall. I try to chat with Megan, words pouring out like a waterfall, but she seems distant, talking mostly about her cheerleader group and their neighborhood drama.

At the mall, Megan says we have to wait by the fountain. A chill runs through me as I remember my nightmare of the chase by that fountain, but I agree. Two girls from school join us, sitting next to Megan, gushing about a beach party last Saturday and how funny Megan was at the movies after. I'm stunned—I wasn't invited, and they all know me. Megan glances at me, hesitant, like she knows I'm hurt, but she doesn't say anything.

The girls want to eat at the food court, and Megan asks if I have any money. I tell her I have a little and not to worry. I order a fountain drink—I'm still full from breakfast—while they get pizza and drinks. They talk among themselves, barely including me, and I wonder why Megan even asked me along. Maybe it's because I pushed for it, not her.

Well, there's no point in feeling bad, so I try to enjoy myself. After eating, we walk around the mall. I stop to window shop, and when I turn, they're gone. I spend an hour looking for them, then head to the payphone by the entrance to call Mom. Before I reach it, I hear Megan calling my name. I turn, and there they are, acting casual. "Where have you been? We've been looking everywhere for you."

I don't believe her—and their faces don't match the story. I just want to go home and focus on horseback riding next week. But I'm stuck with them for another hour or so. Megan talks to me more, but it all feels forced. Maybe she's just trying to keep me from telling her mom, or maybe she's trying to convince me their absence was accidental. I excuse myself and say I'm hungry, heading to the food court alone. As I walk away, I hear the other girls giggle. I glance back, and they stop. Megan looks concerned. I tell her I'll meet them at the entrance in an hour. I eat my teriyaki chicken and fried rice in peace, washing it down with another soda.

I wander the mall alone for the rest of the hour. I feel lighter not having to vie for Megan's attention. I think about school starting, making new friends, and my riding lessons. When the hour's up, I wait by the entrance. Megan walks up, showing me some T-shirts she bought for school. We chat about what she did while I was gone. Her mom picks us up, drops me off, and I hurry inside, avoiding the conversation as our moms talk about today.

I don't expect Megan to call again after this, and I'm not sure I want her to for a while. I go to my room and sit, thinking about what's next. The feelings of depression and disconnect swell, and I feel a need to vent, but to who?

That night, as I drift off, I hear the doorknob open and close again. I black out until morning. When I get dressed in the morning, I notice another bruise, this time on my left leg. I have no memory of hitting anything. It's just another unexplained mark.

The day for horseback riding finally arrives. I wear jeans, sneakers, and a lavender T-shirt, pulling my hair into a ponytail. Mom drives us out, the road winding through woods and the scenery stretching wide. We pull up to a large stable with wooden corrals and pasture fences. Connie greets us, a warm woman who manages the barn. She's my teacher. She introduces me to Betsy, a brown horse, quiet and withdrawn from being ridden by so many students.

I can't help feeling nervous. Betsy's huge up close, and my legs are shaky as I climb on. Connie picks an English saddle, saying it's easier to start with than a Western one. I don't know the difference, but trust her. She walks beside Betsy, guiding her, as I sway atop, gripping on tightly to keep my balance. We circle the corral, getting me used to the height and motion. 'You're doing great," Connie says encouragingly. "You'll be a good rider. Mom watches, snapping pictures with her camera.

I climb down after the lesson, my legs wobbly from the new strain, but I'm eager for more. Connie notices my enthusiasm and smiles. We head home, and I change into jean shorts and head out on my bike—not toward Leslie or Tony but to the other subdivision, searching for solitude.

The trail's quiet until I hear voices. As I near the treehouse, they grow louder. Tony, Leslie, and a mix of kids I don't know are playing baseball in the field beside it. Tony spots me and calls my name, smiling. He asks if I want to join. I look at them—Leslie included—and say I'll pass, not feeling up for it. His smile fades to a frown as I ride by. I wonder if he saw my hurt, if he knows I liked him, but I keep going, needing distance.

I ride around the other subdivision, the quiet soothing me. Guilt creeps in. For some reason, liking Tony feels like cheating, but I'm not married, not attached. It's strange, and I push the feeling aside. School's coming soon. There'll be new friends, hobbies, maybe a way out of this slump. But the isolation bites. I have fewer people to share with now.

A black Dodge Charger pulls up by the trail entrance. It just sits there, tinted windows hiding whoever's inside. A chill hits me. I pedal fast, my bike wobbling as my heart races. I hear the car pull away, honking as it speeds off. I slow, catching my breath, then race home to stash the bike.

I spend the night in the library, reading with Janis in my lap. Depression seeps back in, memories of Megan's warmth haunting me. I hope tomorrow's better. I don't know if not praying is helping, but it has seemed to cut rude people out of my life. Maybe I'll start again tomorrow, reading the Bible, too, and see what happens. I think back to the dream. Were the spaceships, the "I love you," tied to my guilt for liking Tony? Is there something deeper? I drift off, wondering.

CHAPTER 9

*R*odney sits at Nora's dining table, watching as she serves him a bowl of steaming soup. She's cooked crab cakes, stuffed mushrooms, and an upside-down pineapple cake—her favorite—hoping he'll enjoy it. He takes a bite and smiles, telling her it's delicious. She feels a lift but brushes it off, modest.

She tells him it's easy to cook well here, with so many ingredients available, unlike the desert trading post where she grew up. She describes her life there, filled with sand, scarcity, and simplicity. Rodney listens, nodding. "You looked happy there," he says. She pauses, puzzled, and asks how he knew what she looked like back then. He explains he saw her once, passing through as a young girl, and hoped he'd meet her someday. That chance came when he spotted her crossing the street in town, said hello, and started talking. He smiles and says the rest is history. She nods, happy, but wonders when he saw her, unnoticed.

School's creeping closer, and my excitement's fading. Will everyone ignore me there too? I've got a week left before it starts, and I want to make it fun. Maybe I can go the beach or movies with Cherie. My second horseback riding lesson's this week too. I find Cherie and ask if she wants to hit the beach.

"Maybe."

"How about the movies?"

She gives me another maybe, her tone flat. I turn to Mom instead and ask if I can go to the movies alone this week. She seems surprised.

"I just want to relax before school starts again, that's all."

"We'll see. The budget's tight with your riding lessons," she replies. "I'll look at things and see."

I say okay and grab my bike, heading out for a ride, the air sharp against my skin. Tony's outside when I roll by, and he rides up the driveway to say hi.

"How's horseback riding going?"

"How did you know about that?"

"I ran into Megan at the beach with friends, and she told me about it," he says. I feel a twinge of hurt. She was at the beach and didn't invite me. I push it down and tell Tony about my first lesson.

"You haven't been around much," I say pointedly, assuming he's dating Leslie now.

He looks down, frowning, and says, "We broke up."

"Why?" I blurt out, maybe a bit too blunt.

"She's just boring," he complains. "She never wants to do anything, and we don't like the same things."

"I'm sorry," I say as sincerely as I can. "I thought you were good together." He smiles and thanks me.

We ride our bikes down the road together, and he says he's seen a car watching my house recently. "What?" I ask. He describes a classic black Dodge Charger he's seen parked across the street at night—no one gets out, lights off, just sits there, then drives away. My blood runs cold.

"How many times have you seen it?"

"I don't know, five or six." I'm stunned. That's around the same number of times I've heard my doorknob turn and shut as I fall asleep. I ask him to keep a journal of the dates and times he sees that car. He looks confused but agrees, like he wants to ask why. But he holds back the question.

We ride a bit longer, then I head home. Mom says we're going out for ice cream as a treat before school starts. I'm surprised but glad. We pile into the car and drive to the beach. I order a mint chocolate chip waffle cone at a small ice cream shop—my favorite. Mom gets butter pecan, and Cherie gets chocolate. We stroll along the shopfronts, window-shopping, our cones dripping in the heat.

"What would to like to do before school?" Mom asks. Cherie agrees to the movies with me. The ice cream and her yes lift my mood. We wander a bit more, then head home. The next day, Mom schedules my second riding lesson. I wear a pink T-shirt, jeans, and sneakers, and we drive out, the scenery unfolding pretty and wide.

Connie's not outside when we arrive, so I push open the wooden stable door. It opens to a big space. There's an office straight ahead, rows of stalls lining both sides, at least ten rows with two stalls each, twenty on either side of the office. We step into the office. The reception desk is in front and another desk to the left, but there's no Connie and no receptionist. We wait outside, standing in the open area.

Five minutes pass, and Connie hurries in. "I'm so sorry," she apologizes. "The last rider showed up late, and I got here as quickly as I could." She offers us sodas from her office, but Mom and I decline. I start my lesson, this time holding the reins in the corral. It's harder than it looks, guiding Betsy where I want her to go. Connie says I'll switch horses as I improve. Betsy's a starter horse, calm and steady.

After the ride, I try to pet Betsy, but she shies away from me. Connie suggests bringing apples next time to bond with her. "I'll ask Mom," I say. Mom watches from outside the corral as I walk Betsy out with Connie. We say goodbye, Mom pays, and we head home.

That night, I fall asleep thinking about school and hoping things will turn around. I dream I'm in my room, looking out the window. I can see Tony ride by fast with friends, laughing and talking—especially with some neighborhood girls. I watch him for a while, his voice carrying. Then headlights sweep around the house, and a black two-door Dodge Charger pulls up under my window. The driver rolls down his window and yells up at me, "Why do you keep looking at Tony? Do you like him."

I can see him from my second-story view—tall, dark-haired, handsome, with a commanding presence. I tell him it's none of his business and ask why he cares. He gets louder, criticizing Tony. "There nothing special about him, and he's not even good-looking. Why do you keep watching him?"

I start to walk away, weary of his domineering tone. What does it matter to him? He notices and tells me to get in the car. "Why would I do that? I don't even know you." He insists, saying I should stop looking at Tony. "No," I say more urgently, "I'm not getting in." He opens the passenger door, beckoning me inside. I step back from the window, and the dream ends.

I wake up in a cold sweat, wondering why. Morning comes, and I spot another bruise on my right wrist. Once again, I have no idea how it got there. At breakfast, Mom says we're going to the store. As we pull out of the driveway, she stops, noticing tire tracks—someone drove down the driveway, veered left, and kept going. She gets out and follows the tracks. They lead under my bedroom window, then circle back to the street past the kitchen porch. "Did anyone hear anything last night?" she asks quietly. I don't say anything—it was just a dream, not real. I decide to ask Tony if he saw anything when we get back.

After we bet back from the store, I head out on my bike, looking for Tony. He's alone in his front yard, and I roll up, asking if he saw the Dodge Charger last night. He looks at me, confused, and asks what I mean. "You said you saw it parked by my house a few times and agreed to tell me if it showed up again," I remind him.

"I have no idea what you're talking about," he says, tilting his head.

I feel disappointed and uneasy. I insist we just had this conversation. He shakes his head and says it never happened. "Well," I say, "let me know if you see it, OK?" I quickly excuse myself and head off. He watches me riding with a strange look, like I'm unhinged. I decide not to bring it up with him again.

Back home, I walk around the yard, looking for anything odd beyond the tire tracks. Leslie and some neighborhood kids approach. They seem almost threatening and say they've declared war on me. "What? What do you mean? I haven't even been around you guts lately."

They start mocking my clothes, saying I'm not stylish, don't fit in, and I'm not welcome at their houses anymore. I turn and walk inside, done with them. They want a fight, but I won't bite. I never told Leslie I liked Tony— we weren't even close—but did Megan spill the beans? Tony and I aren't dating, just friends. Or is it something else? The dream felt so real, and there are tire tracks as proof. That driver was mad about Tony—and those girls were there, too, in the background.

I decide to steer clear of them, wondering if this'll spill over into school. My breath catches. Is there going to be war at school? Panic rises in me. I go looking for Mom. She's in the living room, and I explain what happened. She looks worried, saying I should be careful because one of the girls might try to fight me. I find that highly unlikely, but I agree to avoid the neighborhood kids for now.

That night, Mom lets Cherie and me go to the movies to take my mind off things. She hasn't told Cherie about the kids, since they haven't said anything to her. We go with Mom in the evening. She buys us popcorn and drinks—a rare splurge. It's pretty clear she feels bad about today. I pick a comedy. I need some laughs to forget all this drama. We enjoy it—well, Mom and I more than Cherie. After it's over, I feel a little better, and we drive home in the warm summer dark, the air soft.

At home, I wonder if I should stop praying and reading the Bible again—things are just getting worse. I decide to pause and ask where God is, why He's letting this happen. I fall asleep crying, hoping for rest and a fresh tomorrow. The bruise on my wrist aches, swollen now.

A few days pass, and it's the first day of school. We file into the auditorium for the principal's speech. I see kids from last year. I know some of them but not others. Megan's there with her new friends. She says hi to me but stays with them. Tony's with the neighborhood crew—I don't go near them. I spot Hanna, a friend from last year, and sit down with her. Megan glances over at me a few times, then quickly looks away. After the speech, I head to first period, announcements crackling over the intercom.

The day drags on forever. Hanna has a different lunch period, so I sit with Ruby, a girl I know a little. She's pretty nice, chats with me, and I join her group. Megan's far off with her own crowd. After lunch, the day picks up. Most of my classes are on the second floor, which I like. Still, loneliness gnaws at me, depression clawing its way back in. I try to look happy, but it's a lie. There's some sort of barrier. I can't connect, and people seem closed off, hostile to me for no reason. I don't feel liked anymore. I miss the old days with Megan, her reassurance, and sharing everything.

CHAPTER 10

*R*odney lifts the diamond ring, its facets catching the light as he tilts it, studying it from up close to as far as his arm can stretch. He wavers between a round solitaire and a princess cut. He likes the round one for Nora, but he's drawn to the elegance of the princess cut, his own taste a bit more sophisticated. Then a third ring catches his eye: a round diamond framed by gold petal leaves. It's perfect for her. He smiles as the clerk slips it into a velvet box and a shopping bag, assuring him he can return with Nora to size it later.

The first week of school flies by as I settle into my new schedule and teachers. Megan's absence stings less now; I've got Hanna and Ruby to talk to. My birthday's coming up, and Mom asks if I want to have a party with school friends. I shake my head. "No, just a dinner out and cake at home."

She agrees, and I feel lighter for opting for something small this year. It's Saturday, and I need to unwind from everything. Next weekend's the party, so Mom wants to plan a bit today.

After my horseback riding lesson, I step out for a walk, but stop short. There are chalk words scrawled across the edge of the driveway: fatso, weirdo, and dork. I grab a broom from the garage and angrily sweep them away, the bristles scraping concrete. I'll have to stay wary and keep watch now. What if they escalate and try to spray paint the house or cars?

I don't tell Mom or Cherie about it. Mom would just ground me so I can't go out alone until this passes. The whole thing is unnerving, but I can't stay cooped up. I take my bike—a faster escape if needed—and head for the other subdivision. Passing Leslie's yard, I see her with the neighborhood girls, staring as I ride by. Leslie's brother, the one who called me a dork once, is my main chalk suspect.

Leslie shouts, "Why are you staring at us?" I wasn't. My eyes were focused ahead, but I pedal even faster to get past them. She mutters to another girl that I started it, that I deserve it. Their shift from friendly to hostile makes no sense; nothing happened. Even Tony's silent now. Why isn't he defending me?

I hit the trail, gliding past the empty treehouse, pedaling quickly to avoid anyone tailing me. What if that strange car's here again? I hope not and push on to the subdivision. It's lined with nice homes. There's a white, modern, single-story one with Oriental-style double doors, big windows, an arch, and French doors off a wrought-iron porch.

A sudden urge pulls me to go inside. What if someone's home? But the feeling swells, sharp and insistent. I pray hard against it, willing the energy to fade. The feeling eases as I ride past. Glancing back, I see a towering shadow, fifteen feet tall, stride from the house, cross the street, and vanish into the woods.

I have a sudden thought. What if you could stretch the space between atoms, making yourself grow huge or shrink small? The porch shadow that attacked me was human-sized. This one's just bigger, but it's familiar. I watch it melt into the trees, then ride on, able to breathe again—the threat's gone.

I admire the homes and head back, slipping past the treehouse where the kids are lingering. I try to stay quiet, but a branch snaps loudly under my tire. Some of the kids look over. One jeers, "Fat Albert!" I race home as fast as I can.

On Monday, I focus on Hanna and Ruby at school, dodging the others and this whole mess. Hanna's friend Stacy joins us. She's the regular class clown, always making jokes, but her jabs can sting. While waiting for class, I tell Hanna I like the red onions on the cafeteria salad. Stacy saunters up, grinning, and says, "That's why your breath's so bad." She laughs while I stare. "Oh come on. Can't you take a joke?"

"I'll laugh when it's funny, not mean," I reply.

This is actually happening a lot lately. I can feel anger flaring up out of nowhere. I try my best to hide it, but my mood shows. There's sadness, too, sudden and deep. I cry for hours, dark thoughts swirling through my head. There's some kind of energy pushing against it, and I let it in.

Finally, the week's over and Saturday arrives—my birthday. I ask for chocolate cake and vanilla ice cream after my lesson. We stop at a pizza place on the beach strip for a late lunch. It's an English tavern-style spot, with an arched wooden door, and gray stone walls. A dim hall opens into a big dining room with heavy tables, red plastic cups glowing in the low light. We order pepperoni and cheese pizzas.

I'm starving, so I dive in while my family chats, barely eating. Dad's here, too, which is rare and pretty nice. The pizza's like lava. I blow on my slice, impatient but remembering past burns.

The waitress refills our Cokes, and I settle into the peace of this place, switching between bites of pepperoni and cheese. After four slices I'm stuffed. We box up the rest and head for home.

There's still some time before the party. I open cards from grandparents —twenty dollars each—and aunts and uncles—ten each. Janis hovers around my feet, her tail wagging and her eyes on me expectantly.

We're laughing when the phone rings. I answer, expecting birthday wishes, but there's only silence. "Hello?" No reply. I hang up. Brushing it off, I rejoin my family in the dining room.

Mom brings out the cake, rich with buttery chocolate frosting. I blow out the candles. She serves me first, a slice of cake and two scoops of ice cream. I savor it, asking for more cake. Then it's time to open gifts: a horse care book, jeans, cowgirl shirts, socks, scrunchies, boots, and a hat from Cherie. I'm thrilled. I'll look so stylish for my lessons.

I lug my haul upstairs, buzzing with excitement, as the others clean up. Sunday, we attend church. Afterward, Mom asks if I'd like to go to the mall to use some of my birthday cash. "I'll think about it," I say. "Either today or next weekend."

I decide on today. We all go, needing the fresh air. I hunt for school outfits, but spot Leslie with her mom. She approaches me. I eye her warily. "I'm sorry for all the weirdness lately," she says softly. "I don't know why I've been acting this way." I accept her apology, puzzled by her flip-flopping, and move on with Mom and Cherie. To be honest, I'm over the instability of the neighborhood crew.

Megan and Tony feel like ghosts now, just distant memories. I find nothing I want to buy and decide to hold off on spending any of my money. My birthday was sweet, and Leslie's truce makes me feel a little better, although I'm not sure the other kids agree.

I go to sleep happy, hoping for some much-needed rest. Rolling over, I drift off but wake with a start to an unexpected presence. Dirt hits my face. I swipe it off, flip on the lamp—nothing's here, just powder on my sheets and cheeks. I wash myself off, wipe the bed, and go back to sleep with the light on. I'm exhausted when I wake up for school the next morning.

English class lifts me a little. We're writing a play about Lincoln and building sets. I volunteer to help make the sets, and I love it. It's a wonderful distraction, and the week flies by, painting and laughing, although the unhappiness lurks just below the surface.

Ruby says she's planning a surprise party and needs to sit with some other kids who will be attending it with her. I shrug, not thinking much about it. But the days pass, and she stays with them and not me. I eat alone outside, feeling isolated and unnoticed. And I'm always so tired despite sleeping.

The next Saturday, after my riding lesson, Mom takes me back to the mall. I snag a black quilted purse with a gold-black chain—taking solace in the small victory. I've had my eye on it for a while.

It's back to school on Monday. Working on the set helps to cheer me up. I smile more, even chatting with the other kids in class. Even Ruby notices, and she comes over to talk to me during PE. "It's nice to see you happy," she says. "You've seemed so depressed lately. It's why I haven't been talking to you as much lately," she admits. It stings. So she's a fair-weather friend. I am starting to see people more clearly now and how self-serving they can be.

When the weekend comes again, I put on my cowgirl gear and head back for another riding lesson. Connie thinks it's cute with my English saddle. I think it would look better with a western saddle, though.

Finally, the day of the play performance arrives. Our set looks great, and I take a lot of pride in the part I played. How do the pros do it? I began pondering what working on Broadway productions or movie sets would be like. Making sets for movies or TV shows would be wonderful as the sets would change often. I could see myself doing it as a career one day.

CHAPTER 11

*R*odney fidgets at Nora's door, his nerves jangling as he pats his
suit pocket, checking the ring box. He's planned a nice evening
at a restaurant—or so she thinks. She answers in a white satin dress and
coat, wearing a turban crowned with peacock feathers pinned by a
turquoise clasp, elegant as jewelry.

The drive's quiet. Nora can feel the tension, unaware of the reason for
his anxiety. She smiles at him, watching traffic and pedestrians roll by as
they near the restaurant.

A live band plays near their table. Nora sways, distracted, while Rodney
orders champagne unobserved. When it arrives, he offers her a glass,
pouring as she nods. With his right hand, he slips the ring onto her finger
while handing her the glass—clumsy, but she laughs, astonished, and it's
enough.

The school year drags on, marked by constant mood swings and restless
nights. Finally, summer break arrives. It's been a tough year. I haven't been
able to maintain any lasting friendships, but maybe, just maybe, I'll make
some real friends next year.

On day one of my break, I sleep in late, waking to pancakes. I feel rested
already. I'm ready for a break, for a great summer. Mom floats the idea of a

waterpark trip. Yes, I'll definitely make the most of this break and just set friends aside for now.

She suggests lunch at the beach and a trip to the strip for some shopping to kick off the summer. I've still got some birthday cash left, so maybe I can buy some sunglasses and even a sundress if it's cheap. As I sit in my room, I ponder outfits. For some reason I've been wanting to dress up more lately. I rifle through my closet looking for a skirt or dress, when I hear a thud rattling the back wall—pipes? An animal? I press my ear close and listen. I hear the wind humming and faint steps creaking up old stairs.

I pull back, stunned. What *is* that? I knock, and the steps stop, like someone's turning toward the sound. Silence follows. I walk out to the hallway and tap the drywall. It feels solid, but I hear a faint stirring coming from the third-floor window, long boarded up. I rush outside to see if the window got open somehow. I check it—no gap, yet the sheer curtains seem to be moving slightly. How can that be, if it's sealed? I hope that no animal has gotten in.

In the library, I listen at the back wall to see if I can hear anything. Sure enough, I can hear whispers, which stop suddenly when I knock. I can hear floorboards squeaking faintly. Someone's definitely there. Cherie walks in, catching me ear-to-wall. "What's up?" she asks.

"Something's in there," I say.

"It's probably a mouse. We can ask Dad to set a trap."

I sink into my recliner to read, but Cherie's curious now, knocking too. As if in answer, there's a loud banging from the other side. She jumps, paling. We lock eyes, both shaken. I return to my book because I'm more used to weird things than she is. Mom calls us to get ready for lunch. I pick out a blue sundress and tan sandals and ask Mom if we can go on a beach walk later.

"Maybe," she says, "but just walking, no swimming."

The drive's sunny and warm. Mom's picked a seafood restaurant. It's in a rustic bungalow with a neon red lobster sign right on the beach. Dad's not a fan of seafood, so it's just us three. The atmosphere's loud, buzzing with tourists fresh off school. Mom seems to enjoy it, but Cherie's still rattled from earlier. I think about teasing her—*welcome to my world*—but she probably wouldn't find it funny.

I order fried fish, coleslaw, and fries. Cherie copies me, while Mom chooses sushi. Our clear glasses gleam in the bright light from big windows. There's a patio in the back spilling onto the beach. Seagulls circle overhead, crying for scraps, while the patio diners laugh and shout.

The food's delicious. We devour it all, not leaving a scrap behind. Mom doesn't seem to be in a hurry to leave and lingers, relaxed, sipping a final refill. After a while, we leave a tip and head out, checking out some accessory shops for sunglasses. We window-shop first, skipping one with dull displays, then enter a second. It's hard because I see so many pairs I like, but I finally pick one, fighting off an unexpected, fierce urge to steal it. I pray in silence, and the urge fades. I pay for the sunglasses, relieved.

We walk the beach, my new shades on, watching seagulls skitter, their legs a blur. The warm breeze carries the scent of the ocean, which I find calming. After a nice, slow stroll, we head to the car and drive home, the radio on, and my mind on tomorrow's riding lesson.

I stay up late. It's the first day of summer after all. But as I fall into sleep, I start dreaming about a man chasing me through woods, his knife gleaming. I dodge branches, my heart pounding, until Cherie's knock wakes me. "Help me find Janis—she's gotten out," she says. She's wearing a strange, old-fashioned dress. It seems like something from the 1940s. "My friend's here to drive us," she adds.

Uneasy, I try to stall her. "I'll be down soon. I need to put on shoes." I go to check Cherie's room—and find her inside asleep. I wake her and ask if she was downstairs. "Of course not!" she snaps. I go back to my room and lock my door, leaving the lamp on.

The next day at my lesson I'm exhausted, yawning hugely in my cowgirl hat and shades. Connie doesn't notice. After we're done, she mentions a horse for sale. It's only $400, a brown horse with a light mane. The owner has to sell because they're moving to New York. I beg my Mom. "Ask your father," she says, "but no promises." I'm giddy at the thought, praying that it'll be mine.

Over dinner, I pitch Dad hard on the idea. "It's a family investment."

He smiles and says, "I'll think about it." In my mind, it's a done deal, and I start planning my cowgirl life.

The night brings more strangeness. A thud jerks me awake. I get up and go into the hallway to check on things. Cherie's light's on. I creep over and knock. She cracks the door open and peeks at me. She's fine but dazed. "Look at this."

She points me toward an old wedding dress in her closet. "Where'd you get that?" I ask.

"I had a nightmare. I was getting married to a monster. When I woke up," she says with a haunted look, "they were just there."

I see there's a gold ring on her dresser too. I reach out to touch it, and it burns my hand. I drop it, recoiling, as Cherie just stares vacantly. I run into my room and lock my door. I keep the lamp on, and my sleep is fitful.

In the morning, I go to Cherie's room. I ask her about the dress and the ring. She looks at me in confusion. "What dress? What ring?" I tell her about last night, about her nightmare. "You must have dreamed it," she insists, showing me her empty closet and jewelry box. I leave her room, confused but unconvinced.

A few days later, Dad says he's got some good news for us. I'm excited, waiting to hear that he's getting the horse. But that's not it. No, he found a used motorboat. Cherie cheers while I slump in disappointment. "What's the problem?" he asks. "I've wanted one forever." Understanding dawns as he studies my face. "Maybe we'll get a horse later," he says, but it's not convincing at all.

I go up to my room to sulk. Janis begs to come in, so I open the door. She curls up on my lap, and petting her soft head makes me feel a little bit better. I think about how I can make my horse ownership dream come true and spend some time in the library before heading off to sleep.

CHAPTER 12

$\mathcal{N}$ora beams at Rodney, eager to introduce him to her mother. She's always dreamed of getting married in the small desert church she attended as a child. He listens to her vision and grins. "Let's do it there." She glows with joy, admiring her engagement ring. She urges him to meet her mom as soon as possible.

Mom says she's taking us to the store to help Dad today. I groan inside. It's dull there. We always get stuck in the back office while they work. I pack a book, and Cherie brings drawing stuff to help pass the time.

After breakfast, I dress in some capris, a navy T-shirt, and matching sneakers, my hair in a ponytail. I need a fresh look, so I'm growing my hair out longer. We head out to my parent's rustic feed store. It's called Caring For All Of Creation, and they sell fruit trees, veggies, garden goods, bird-baths, planters, rabbit ornaments, and so many other things. I sure would like some fruit trees at home. Maybe a rabbit, too, someday.

Inside, the shopping carts are on the left, the checkout's straight ahead, and the seed displays are on the right. The feed shelves stretch out, flanked by farm and beekeeping supplies. I wander around the store, thinking about adding beekeeping to my hobbies. Dad greets me, but we get cut off by a customer with a question about fruit trees.

I head to the back office. It's a spartan room with a cement floor, maple desk, faux leather chair, filing cabinets, couch, and end table. I sigh and settle in. Mom brings us Cokes, pretzels, and napkins from the desk. "Just holler if you need something," she says. I give her a thumbs up as she heads out front.

The office phone rings. "Ignore it," says Cherie. "It's the business line." But the ringing doesn't stop. That's odd. I answer, and there's nothing but silence.

"Hello?" No response. I hang up. It's the number my parents give out to business associates, not customers. We sip on our Cokes, munch pretzels, and enjoy the AC. Actually, it works so well I'm a little chilly. I lounge on the couch reading while Cherie draws at the desk.

After a while, Mom pops in. "We'll be going home soon. Dad's help arrived." I'm pretty happy—the recliner sure beats this couch. When she returns, we grab our stuff and head out to the car. Cherie seems fidgety and a little anxious. Why?

The drive's peaceful enough. There's no traffic, and everything seems normal until I feel a prickling. The presence again. I look at the side mirror and see a black car following us closely, aggressively. Mom seems oblivious, humming along to the radio. The car rides our tail. She sees it, holding steady, waiting for it to pass. It zips around us, and I can see it—a Dodge Charger, with two shadowy figures inside. They stare at me as they zoom past. Mom just seems relieved they're not behind us anymore. But there's another car coming toward us from the other direction. My heart leaps. Are they going to crash? Suddenly, the Charger shifts sideways in an impossible way, avoiding the crash. It drives off ahead and then just vanishes into thin air. The other driver doesn't even seem to see it. I'm stunned.

"Did you see that, Mom? It just disappeared!"

"No, it just sped off," more says with a frown.

"But you had to see that," I insist. "It just, just slid sideways and then disappeared!"

"It was just a near-miss," Mom answers tightly, looking at me strangely.

When we get home, I make myself a ham and cheese sandwich and pour a glass of milk. Janis sits with me at the nook. Cherie comes down while I'm eating, giving me a chance to check on her. "You okay?" I ask.

"Fine, just tired," she says.

That night, I feel the prickling again, the presence of someone or something watching me. I lock my door and turn off the lamp. I pull my covers up tightly and drift off thinking about my dork book. I haven't used it since that time with Megan. Maybe I'll show Cherie because she likes to draw too.

In my dream, I'm canoeing on a camping trip. The water begins to shake, tipping the boat. There's an alligator swimming toward me. I steady the canoe the best I can and paddle with all my might, but it keeps getting closer. It lunges up to grab me and—I wake, door ajar, footsteps in the hall. Mom calls, "You okay? I heard screaming." She peers in, asking why I'm on the bed's edge.

"I'm lying down."

"I know you're sitting there, but all I can see are your eyes and hair," she insists. The image fades as I rise. I'd locked the door, hadn't I?

Mom's genuinely concerned and suggests I sleep somewhere else for the night. We head for the guest room near her bedroom, where she can hear me and be there if I need her. I take my pillow, clock, and blanket, wary after that whole mix-up with Cherie. The guest room's pretty bare, and I'm still spooked so I barely sleep.

I drag myself out of bed in the morning and head back to my room. There's a fresh bruise on my upper right arm. I touch it gingerly and recoil in pain. Mom tells me to come to the guest room from now on anytime I have bad dreams. I agree and go outside to grab my bike. I need to get out of the house. At least I have a riding lesson later.

That night I'm exhausted and crash early. In my dream, I'm floating in a clear rock pool, warm and calm, looking up at the sky. Suddenly, the ground starts to shake and the ground under the pool breaks apart. I start to sink, pulled under, struggling to swim but unable to break free. I wake with a start and see something skittering on my window—a cat? A huge scorpion? But it was walking on the glass, and they can't do that. What was watching me in my sleep?

At breakfast, Mom suggests a waterpark day. Cherie and I leap at the idea, dressing fast after breakfast and scrambling into the car with our things. As we get close, I can see blue tube slides towering over the chaotic crowd. Happy kids are darting everywhere, their parents chatting. The air is filled with the scents of chlorine and sunscreen. Mom's dressed in her straw sun hat and shades. "Well, what do you girls want to do first?"

"Tube rides!" I exclaim. The stairs are long, and the sun's hot, but it is so worth it.

Five stories up, Cherie is the first to go. She zips off with a little scream. I go next. It's a lot steeper than it looks, and I'm a blur on the way down. I hit the runway, giddy, sliding to a stop. Mom joins us, laughing.

We decide to float on the lazy river next. We spend a good hour bobbing in our tubes in the slow current. I dunk my head under once, but it's like swimming in sunscreen, and I vow never to do that again. When we finally hop out of our tubes, we decide to go on the whitewater raft ride. It's like a roller coaster on water, and we bounce and splash our way through the whole thrilling ride.

"We should get lunch," Mom suggests, "before the restaurant gets too crowded." We agree and follow her to the open-air spot and sit at a table with a big umbrella for shade. Lunch is pizza slices and sodas. I eat slowly, watching people and hoping no one I know comes by. Though if I'm being honest, I miss Megan.

More rides follow. I feel good here, safe. Maybe it's the daylight and my family that ease me. It's a wonderful day, though. When we get home, I sip lemonade on the porch, Janis beside me, watching butterflies. "Hello there," says Dad, heading inside. I know what I'm going to doodle in my dork book tonight—Mr. Peanut at the waterpark.

Just as I'm getting up to go in for dinner, I hear an engine roaring. I turn to look, and I see a black Dodge Charger sitting across the street. As I gawk at the car, it peels out, tires smoking, the stench of burning rubber filling my nostrils. Janis whines, pawing at the door. I can hear the sound of the engine fading away as the Charger roars down the road.

CHAPTER 13

*O*ora watches the desert scenery as Rodney drives them toward her mother's house, a chance to introduce him at last. He says it's a fine excuse to take his car beyond the city, as the gas mileage is much better on open roads. She's arranged a bouquet of flowers, small gifts, and a picnic basket in the backseat for her mom. The drive is long, and Nora is eager to arrive.

Rodney hides his nerves as they draw closer, but tension simmers beneath his calm exterior. After several hours, they pull up to a small adobe house, its whitewashed walls glowing inside and out, a courtyard fountain gurgling softly. A horse grazes in a field, with a narrow river cutting through. At the sound of their arrival, Pearl, Nora's mother, steps outside, greeting them with a smile. Rodney shakes her hand eagerly. Pearl's eyes flick to a necklace tucked into his shirt. He meets her gaze, and they exchange an unspoken thought, while Nora remains oblivious.

Summer has slipped away, and school is just around the corner. I'm not really nervous this time; I just want to get through it as quickly as I can. Mom, Cherie, and I do our back-to-school shopping at the mall. I'm especially drawn to bright floral patterns. I have my heart set on a metal band watch, and Mom promises she'll get it for my birthday. And a new ring, too, since I lost the old one.

I'm starting high school in a new district. Mom allowed the change after all the drama last year. Today marks the first day, and some doubts creep in. I miss the old school's familiar rhythm and faces. This place feels foreign. It's an old brick building, single-storied, with rows of classrooms linked by covered walkways. Large windows line the back walls, chalkboards up front, all painted a faded green. The desks are worn with age. Honestly, I like the old school better, but maybe the kids here will be nicer.

History class opens the day, and I like the teacher. I meet someone new, Bianca, who sits behind me. She shares my love for history and books. As the day goes by, things are going pretty well. I head home feeling better than I thought I would. This is the weekend Dad's picking up the motorboat, and he's eager to show it off to Cherie and me. I do my best to muster up some enthusiasm, though my heart still pines for a horse. Cherie and Dad are brimming with excitement. Mom stays more even-keeled.

In celebration of our first day, Mom prepares a special dinner—home-made lasagna. The warm, savory scent fills the house. She sets it on the table along with breadsticks and salad, steam rising in delicate curls. Janis hovers at my feet, pleading for a taste. I slip into the kitchen for a plate, placing a small bit down for her, and she settles in happily beneath the table.

The long day weighs on me, and I long for sleep. It's the first day, so there's no homework to keep me up. I retreat to the library with a book, but my calm is broken by that prickling feeling. I'm being watched again. Janis erupts into loud barks, fixating on the entrance to the room, where I sense the presence. I quickly get up and head downstairs to my room.

The school week passes in a blur. Today's my horseback riding lesson, after which the boat will arrive. As Mom and I prepare to go, I spot two large, gift-wrapped boxes near the piano in the living room. "Who are those for?"

She smiles coyly and says, "It's a surprise for later." I assume they have something to do with the motorboat and let it drop.

At the stable, I discover that Hanna's family has bought the horse I wanted, and they're moving it to a stable closer to their home. Connie's voice carries a touch of sadness as she tells us they'll pick it up today. I focus on barrel racing during my lesson, trying to brush my disappointment aside. Back home, those boxes nag at me. I ask Mom about them for the millionth time, but she's waiting for the boat to arrive to answer. Hours later, it rolls in —a sleek white craft on a tow rig, easing into the water at our dock. Dad and Cherie climb aboard, exploring the controls. I linger briefly, my interest thin.

When we head back inside, I ask about the boxes again. Dad chuckles. "Go ahead, open them."

"Is it a family gift?" I ask.

"Well, that depends on how much you embrace it."

I tear off the wrapping. The first box contains an eight-frame beehive and starter kit.

"I know you wanted the horse," he explains, "and maybe we can get one later. I hope this is suitable for now. I've seen how you linger over the bee keeping supplies at the store." He's right, and I wrap him in a hug.

"Thank you so much!"

"I'll help you set it up," he promises.

The second box holds more supplies. Relief washes over me. This is a hobby of my own! Mom grins and says, "I'll expect plenty of honey for my tea and warm milk."

Dad says we'll have to wait until spring to get started—it's too late this year—and Mom suggests we get Italian honeybees, which are common here. Dad agrees and says we can do it. We carry the boxes to the garage, and I glance back with a big grin, imagining hives humming with life.

The weeks at school unfold, and I grow closer to Bianca. She invites me to her Halloween sleepover with some other girls. I'm touched by her inclusion and immediately accept.

A week later, there's a new girl in my history class. She sits a row left of Bianca and me. I offer her a smile, but she doesn't return it. During free time, I turn to chat with Bianca, and I can sense the girl's eyes on me. I let it slide and move on with my day.

Saturday, Dad takes us boating on a winding river path. It's way more thrilling than I'd expected. He makes sharp turns, Mom and Cherie squeal-ing, playing up their excitement. I can see wildlife darting along the banks— deer, birds—alive in ways I had never noticed before. Dad races toward home, swinging around in a big U-turn that sends a wave splashing back as he docks.

I rush inside to change for my lesson and then come down to wait for Mom in the foyer.

"Did you have fun on the boat?" she asks.

I nod sincerely. "Yes! I hope we can do it again tomorrow."

After my lesson, Connie asks if I'd like to sign up for rides on a trail through the woods and on a private beach. "It's free," she says.

"I'll ask my parents," I reply eagerly. When I see Mom, I tell her about it, and she loves the idea.

Monday, after history, I catch the new girl—Jasmine, not new it turns out, just transferred classes—talking about me with some of my classmates, her tone cutting. I ask Bianca about it later. She tells me Jasmine's a popular girl and that she misinterpreted my first-day chat with her as gossip. Bianca clarified I hadn't mentioned her, but Jasmine wouldn't listen, and she's been spreading venom since. "I'm sorry," Bianca says, "I forgot to tell you."

I feel sick to my stomach knowing Jasmine's been talking about me this whole time, turning the other kids against me. I'm starting to like horses and dogs much more than people.

I don't tell Mom about it, hoping it just goes away. According to Bianca, it's not even worth trying to talk to Jasmine about it. I feel a familiar sense of depression, my mood shifting. I tell myself I'll bring it up if it gets any worse.

I still go to Bianca's party on Friday. I show up a little late, dressed as a lumberjack. Everyone seems to admire my outfit. They're huddled over a Ouija board, trying to call spirits. I opt out. Then they start a chant trying to make someone levitate. Bianca's mom watches on unbothered, as if this is standard Halloween behavior. It unsettles me.

I stay the night, but a fight fractures the group, with girls picking sides against each other. After breakfast in the morning, Mom shows up to take me home. I tell her about the Ouija board and the weird chants. She's also unimpressed. "Well that's strange."

When we get home, I unpack my things. I find myself missing Megan. I wonder what her Friday was like. This experience has put me off Halloween parties, and I think I'll just avoid them in the future.

Next weekend, I ride the wooded trail. The horses are from a wealthy family's stable. I guess this is a regular event for Connie's clients. I savor the escape, just being outside and riding in nature. For now school is just a distant thought—I just want the year to be done. In fact, I dread going back to school. Even Leslie and those neighborhood jerks were better than Jasmine.

The ride ends, and the horses go back into the stable. Mom's there waiting for me, and we head out for home. I can feel Monday looming, and the stress tightens in my chest. I don't think I can hold all this inside. I need to tell someone soon.

The week crawls by, and I notice my classmates glaring at me for no reason. Turns out one of the girls from the sleepover is in my English class, and she's spreading all sorts of bad things about me. Of all things, she says I'm vain because of my haircut. I like my haircut.

One day she corners me in science. The teacher's nowhere to be seen, and she accuses me of challenging her to fight. She stares at me menacingly but backs off and sits down when the teacher returns.

I really need to talk to someone about all this, so I decide to visit the counselor. Surprisingly, she believes me and handles the bullying situation. The girls involved get in trouble, and for a while, the harassment ends. It feels like a heavy weight has been lifted off my chest. Maybe I can finish the year after all. Maybe I can start sleeping better with the stress reduced.

Things settle down for a while. I turn my attention to bee keeping, reclaiming a stolen joy. I look forward to the horseback ride at the beach next weekend. It's nice to think about things I like instead of school drama.

As I lie in bed, I imagine the beach. I've never seen the private part, and I wonder what it's like. Sleep takes me, but I jolt awake, sitting up suddenly, my heart racing. I don't know what's happened. There's no lingering dream. I flip on the lamp—nothing. I leave it glowing, wondering what caused me to wake up like that. I should have Janis sleep in here with me to alert me if there's any trouble.

Morning comes, and as I dress, I discover another bruise on my right forearm. I need answers—something's wrong, and I have to find out what's going on.

CHAPTER 14

$\mathcal{N}$ ora glances at her mother while Rodney wanders off, studying the desert plants scattered across the dry expanse. She asks her mother what she thinks of him. Catalina's tone hardens as she tells Nora he is not the man she believes him to be. A flicker of confusion crosses Nora's face, and she presses her mother to explain. Catalina speaks of witches from the reservation, recalling how her ancestors, healers on their ancestral land, fought against dark forces wielding unnatural abilities and forbidden knowledge. She warns that such beings can alter their appearance to deceive anyone. That blond, blue-eyed man, she adds, could never hail from their homeland near the reservation. Nora stands there, stunned into silence, her mind racing as Rodney casts a discreet glance back at them. Catalina meets his gaze with a steady stare, then declares she forbids their marriage. Nora tilts her head toward the sky, helpless, as quiet tears slip down her cheeks.

Time moves quickly, and it's nearly spring. Dad has been teaching me to drive the motorboat. I've come to cherish these outings with him and Janis, who delights in the rush of wind across the water. Cherie and Mom prefer to stay behind at the house. I never would have guessed it, but the boat has become a welcome distraction from the weight of school.

We're also working on preparing the beehives, setting up two in case one fails to thrive. I join Dad in assembling the frames and hive boxes, then help construct a stand to lift them off the ground. The metal tops will shield them from rain. We still need nuc boxes—small containers with about 10,000 bees and a caged queen—which are only available from spring to early summer. My white bee suit, which has a mesh hood and covers me from head to toe, waits alongside the smoker, its gentle puffs designed to calm the bees by dulling their alarm pheromones. I spend more time outdoors now, tending a garden too. I've persuaded my parents to plant fruit trees and vegetables this spring, counting on the bees to pollinate them.

School remains a lonely place. I exchange words with a few classmates, but that's about it. It could be worse, I guess—silence beats malice—so I keep to myself, pouring my energy into my own pursuits rather than seeking a circle of friends.

My weekly horseback riding lessons continue on Saturdays. I still dream of owning a horse, and I'm pretty confident I have a good plan to make it happen. I intend to ask Dad if I can work at the store and save up my earnings to buy a horse. I'll suggest building a fence and a small stable here at home.

Life feels like it's taking shape again after a long, hollow spell. However, loneliness lingers, even with family around. I miss having a friend to share trips to the movies or the mall.

Most evenings, I retreat to the library, settling into my recliner with a book while Janis rests at my feet. Lately, she follows me everywhere, a constant shadow. Her presence comforts me.

It's a peaceful Friday evening. The house lies still, the second-floor hallway lights casting a soft warmth as spring begins to tease the air. I cradle a mug of hot tea, moving from my bedroom toward the library. As I pass, I notice that the painting at the end of the hallway is hanging crooked again. I pause to straighten it, then slip back to my room for a pair of house slippers to keep my feet warm before returning to read.

When I step out again, the painting has tilted once more. A chill settles over me. Is something here, knocking it askew? I approach slowly and adjust it back to center, but it slips from the wall, crashing to the floor with a sharp crack. Startled, I worry my parents will think I knocked it down by mistake. I debate leaving it there to show it fell on its own, the frame needing repair, but curiosity draws me to check the right-hand corner for that hidden paper. I turn it over, finding the frame split, and carefully pry it open to reveal a brittle, yellowed sheet folded three times, as if it once fit a long-lost envelope.

I carefully unfold it, revealing elegant cursive in black ink addressed to future descendants. Unease twists in my chest, but I press on. At first I distract myself by gazing at how beautiful the letter appears.

Greetings, my darling descendants,

I know I have told the family my name is Beatrice, but it is Nora. I changed it when I left Arizona to escape my pursuers and rebuild my life. I married Rodney, believing him to be a good man, until I discovered his true nature and broke my vows. Rodney has a brother nicknamed Niffin, who vowed to destroy me and my family for abandoning Rodney. Once leaving, these things began to happen to me: strange things herald their presence—shadows that speak, an unseen gaze bent on harm, items vanishing, people turning against you without cause. I urge you to find Niffin's altar, which has items of our family he uses for black magic, and destroy it. I love you all, and you must hurry for the family's sake.

P.S. The man in the portrait is Rodney, who, in his altered form, resembles Niffin, though without his brother's cruelty.

With all my love, Nora

Stunned, I reassemble the frame and leave it on the floor as if it fell naturally, then tuck the letter into my dresser drawer. What does altered *form* mean? I think back to the two shadows in that black car that passed Mom and me, vanishing into nothing. Was it Rodney, not Niffin, lingering at the store, his pain palpable, mourning Nora and the lineage she created with another man, our great-grandfather, Niffin must be the one hunting us, her descendants.

I feel sadness, worry, then resolve as I process what I've read. I need to find that altar and dismantle it. I wonder what Nora was like, and Rodney, too, and what rift tore such pain through them all. The fact that she kept his portrait suggests some lingering affection.

I wait for my parents to notice the fallen painting, but they pass by without a word. When I check, I see it hanging up again, transformed into a portrait of a young blonde woman with blue eyes, her hair in a bun circled by flowers like a halo, dressed like a ballerina on a floral stool. The frame's not damaged, as if it never fell. What in the world? I resolve to visit the library tomorrow and follow up on the clues Nora left behind.

In my dream that night, I'm walking beside Mom through a desert field with tall grasses and shrubs woven into the rocky soil. A mountain rises ahead, its cliff face carved with pueblo dwellings, a dirt road alive with tourists exploring them. It feels like I'm peering into a memory, but not my own—a place that once thrived, now faded yet enduring, heavy with loneliness and regret.

At breakfast, I ask Mom if I can go to the library to do some research.

"Sure," she says, assuming it's for school, and offers to drop me off before my riding lesson and return later. After lunch, she drops me off at the library. It's a charming gray-brick building framed by dogwood and willow trees, its large windows glinting beyond glass double doors. I start in the "S" section for shadows, then reconsider, drifting to "P" for paranormal activity.

The librarian notices my indecision and asks if I need any help. I hesitate, but she presses gently. I admit I'm seeking material on talking shadows. She tilts her head and asks if these shadows might be shape-shifters. I pause. Transforming *could* mean shape-shifting, and I nod, saying it's possible. She directs me to look under "N" for Navajo witch, leading me to two books on the subject. "Do you know much about it?" I ask.

"A little," she says.

"Is it possible for there to be an item that's broken one minute, then not be broken but changed to something different?" The words sound a little crazy in my ears.

"Hmm, a spell might explain that," she says seriously. She suggests that maybe someone could be immune to the enchantment and see it in its original form.

I think back to that shadow wondering how I could see it at all. Maybe I have some kind of immunity that lets me see the original portrait while others only see the ballerina, concealing Nora's letter. But where could this altar she mentioned be hidden? Questions swirl through my mind with all this new information about Nora and Rodney.

When I turn to ask another question, the librarian has slipped away. I look around for her, but I can't find her. I check out the two books and wait outside for Mom, feeling eyes upon me. Across the parking lot, I see a black crow with bluish-green eyes perched on a bumper block, watching me in silence.

Mom pulls up to the curb by the library's front doors, and I climb in, slipping the books into my backpack. "How'd it go?" she asks. "Did you find what you need for your research?"

I nod, keeping it vague, and she assumes it has to do with school, showing little curiosity. As we drive to the stables under a cool, sunny sky, I look forward to riding, hoping Mom won't peek inside my bag. She lingers by the corral to watch—my secret stays safe.

After the lesson, we bid Connie goodbye and head home. I'm worried that Mom might ask about my research, so I steer our conversation elsewhere. When we get home, I carry the library books to my room and hide them beneath clothes in my dresser drawer. It feels deceptive, but I can't reveal this yet, not with so little to go on, especially if it's some kind of dark family secret.

I don't even know Rodney's last name or his origins beyond Arizona. He could be anyone. And who's the ballerina masking their portrait? I head downstairs to find Mom at the dining table, sorting some store paperwork. I ask about the ballerina, wondering how she's tied to our family. Mom shrugs. "I'm not sure. Maybe a distant relative, a friend of Beatrice's, or it could just be a painting she bought because she liked it." It seems to be the only portrait whose story she doesn't know, kept simply because it was her grandmother's.

Her indifference tells me she's not attached to it, so I head back upstairs to read the library books. As I pass by, I glance at the portrait—it's Nora and Rodney again. I must be seeing through the spell. Why didn't whoever enchanted it simply destroy the letter?

I settle in my room to start the books when I hear a woman's voice calling out "Bernadette," sharp and sudden, from nowhere. It jars me, and I scan the room for any sign of someone. Faint creaking rises from the hallway floorboards. I open my door to look. No one's there, but there's a strand of dark blonde hair lying on the floor. It's the wrong shade and too long to be Cherie's.

I feel something, a presence hovering nearby and watching me. I hurry downstairs to join Mom in the dining room, hoping it'll pass. As I walk down the kitchen steps, the floorboards creak again behind me.

CHAPTER 15

*C*hurch bells echo through the valley, drawing people to gather. The old white adobe church, built in the 1600s, stands small and simple, its interior painted white. A long hallway greets visitors, leading from a modest entrance and branching into a few rooms. To the left lies the sanctuary, where an alcove sits behind a small podium, and beside it, a shallow baptism pool is carved into the floor—too shallow for an adult to submerge fully. Pews stretch toward the back, their wood darkened slightly from years without air conditioning in the desert heat. White lilies and red roses adorn the space. There are garlands draped over pew tops, bouquets on plant stands circling the podium, and a grand white ribbon tied across it.

Nora paces in a back room, preparing herself, her nerves taut, knowing her mother won't attend or bless this marriage. It's the happiest day of her life, shadowed by the deepest sorrow. Rodney's voice steadies her, promising they'll always be a family, and that's the only thing that matters. She glances at her engagement ring, her intricate lace wedding dress catching the light, and smiles, clinging to his words with all her heart.

I enjoy spending my afternoon sitting on the porch drinking lemonade with my family as spring arrives. Afterward, we spent the rest of the evening playing board games together. I began to feel tired as I yawn and excuse myself. I climb the stairs to my room, ready for sleep. I settle into bed, hoping for a restful night, though a faint unease tugs at me as I drift off.

In my dream, I find myself at a masquerade ball, surrounded by guests in exquisite masks—everyone but me. I approach a woman and ask who I am. She turns away, irritation flashing in her eyes. I try speaking to a man next, but he ignores me too. The castle sprawls grandly around me, its halls immaculate, a long table laden with fancy desserts, fruits, and delicate finger foods stretching through the room.

Loneliness presses in—I don't belong here. I just want to know who I am before I leave. A man gestures shyly, beckoning me closer, and whispers that the answer lies in the tower. I thank him and start toward it, but obstacles arise—guests chatter, pulling me toward other corners of the party, or I lose my way, asking for directions that no one will give. At last, a man slips me a note with instructions and vanishes into the crowd before I can thank him.

I reach the tower stairs, but they tremble beneath me, growing more unsteady as I climb. The structure begins to crumble, and I race upward, desperate to find my answer before it collapses. I near the top when the steps give way, and I plummet with the tower's ruins.

I wake with a feeling of falling, heavy with sadness from the dream. Night still cloaks the room. I roll over, yearning for more sleep. As I drift off again, a male voice calls my name. I dismiss it as a dream's echo and try to rest. Ten minutes later, it rings out again, clear, waking me fully. I hear footsteps pacing near my closet, and I can see a human-sized shadow looming, watching me in my bed. My skin crawls as it shifts back and forth, checking to see if I'm awake.

Fear roots me in place. The shadow waits, expecting me to fall back asleep. My heartbeat quickens as I weigh my options. Turning on the lamp might reveal it, the light giving me the upper hand. I lie still, trying to gather my courage, listening to it shifting its weight impatiently.

With a sudden lunge, I flip on the lamp, screaming as I move. I whip around to where the shadow stood—there's nothing there. Light floods the room, and I notice my dresser drawer ajar, the one with the library books. I check inside. The books are still there, shifted slightly, as if the shadow rifled through them.

I settle back into bed, pondering the meaning of my dream, especially that word, "tower." Morning can't come soon enough. I ache to unravel this mystery and banish this shadow, this presence for good. I leave the lamp on through the night.

When dawn comes, I switch it off and head downstairs for breakfast, thinking about what the dream could mean. Alone, I pour a bowl of cereal, feeling curiously rested despite the night's chaos. I decide to check the beehives today and maybe join Dad for a boat ride.

Upstairs, I pull my bee suit and gloves from the closet, carrying them to the kitchen porch and setting them on the nearest chair. In the garage, I grab the hive scraper, smoker, and a bag of pine needles, stuffing them into the smoker to light later with a torch. I haul everything back to the porch, laying it next to my suit.

My riding boots will shield me under the bee suit as I prepare to open the hives. I wedge the scraper between the lid and box, prying them apart— the bees seal it with propolis, a type of glue they make to close gaps in their natural homes.

I lift the lid, resting it atop the second hive, and gently ease the frames apart. Burr comb—honeycomb-linking frames—clings with propolis along the edges, so I move carefully. I examine each frame, studying the queen's egg patterns, noting the brood, capped cells, nectar, and honey, scanning for hive beetles or disease.

Both hives are thriving this week. I plan to make splits next week to ease crowding—a new queen will emerge and either stay or leave with half the colony. Dad's out to fetch a third hive, buoyed by our success. Bees hum around me as I work; I squeeze the smoker, releasing calming plumes to quiet their alarm pheromones.

I finish and close the second hive, gather my tools, and return to the porch. I shed the suit, stow the gear in the garage, then carry the suit and gloves upstairs.

Dad's in the kitchen. "Would you like to go fishing with me and Cherie?" he asks.

"Sure," I agree. He grins, telling me to meet at the dock in five minutes. I stash my gear, swap my boots for sandals, and grab a pair of sunglasses and a sunhat.

At the dock, Dad's set up a cooler and lawn chairs, and a radio's humming softly. He's in a cheery mood. Cherie's already there fishing, her pole in the water. As I watch her beside him, dark feelings surge—resentment, anger, a sudden sense she's an attention-seeker. I'm confused by the feelings. I've never felt this way toward her.

The emotions twist into dislike, unfamiliar, and sharp. I question them, and I feel a fierce energy pressing against me, urging me to embrace the feeling. I resist, and it fights, trying to sway me, but I break free. I breathe heavily, my heart pounding, reeling from what just happened.

Could this be why friends turned on me? Were they hit by the same force, twisting their hearts? It felt like some kind of telepathy, and I know the shadow's behind it. But why target Cherie? It's scheming, turning others against me or me against them.

The entity's presence lingers faintly, eavesdropping on my thoughts, stalking my life. It's some kind of supernatural hunter. I need it gone. Glancing at Cherie, I can see the sadness in her; she's struggling too. The shadow wants me to wound her further, but I won't. I approach her. "How are you holding up," I ask gently.

She shrugs, admitting to feelings of depression and anger. "Have you seen anything odd at home?" I ask. She hesitates, and then Dad interrupts before she can answer, suggesting a boat ride since the fishing's slow. He smiles, oblivious to everything.

We pack up, board the boat, and Dad pulls away from the dock, speeding around the first bend. Wind whips at my hair. The river mirrors the trees in serene beauty before we churn it up, scattering the wildlife. I keep waiting for a moment alone with Cherie, but it never comes.

Nature's calm helps to soothe me, but Cherie's lost in thought. Something's obviously wrong. I wish Dad had brought Janis. Actually, I wonder why he didn't bring her.

Ahead, a rod-like shape bobs in the water. Dad nearly hits it, the boat lurching. He stops, circling back, but whatever it was is gone when we reach the spot. "Did you see that?" he asks. Cherie and I both nod yes, but there's nothing there now.

As we pull away, my gaze drifts to the forest. A woman stands there, her back to me, before a tree. She's wearing a black robe, and her long blonde hair is striking, even from afar. She turns, watching us, still as a statue. I wonder if I'm imagining her, turning to ask Cherie. But when I look back, the woman's gone.

Did I imagine the whole thing? Or did she try to wreck us? I only saw her from a distance, but she reminds me of the ballerina from the painting. I can't be sure, but it seems suspicious.

That night, I sleep with the lamp on again. Morning brings sunshine and birdsong. I head downstairs, wondering if Mom's up because she said she wanted to go to the store early today. Her door's ajar, so I peek in. I gasp at what I see: a blonde woman in a black robe hovers over her, four feet above, staring at Mom while she sleeps. It's the same woman from the river.

The silence hangs heavy. Is she planting dreams or spying? "Mom!" I call. In a blink, the woman's gone.

Mom stirs at my voice. "Thanks for waking me. I'd forgotten the time."

I shut her door and check the painting—still Nora and Rodney, not the ballerina. Janis pads up to me, and I scoop her into my arms, heading down to the kitchen. Over cereal, I think about all I've seen. The shared dreams with Mom suggest that something or someone is meddling in our lives—maybe that woman or the shadow—hovering over us and trying to plant thoughts in our minds.

Janis naps as I finish my breakfast. I step outside for a walk, but Mom descends, ready to head to the store. I blurt out my wish to work there, to save up for a horse. Surprised, she promises to ask Dad today. I wish her a good day, and she walks away with a grin, leaving Cherie in charge.

CHAPTER 16

$\mathscr{N}$ora and Rodney stroll along their usual desert path, passing a mountain with pueblo cliff dwellings. Grasses and shrubs line the trail, its gentle rises and dips perfect for walking. Rodney bought a house nearby—a retreat from the city—close to the church where they wed five years ago. Their daughter, Elizabeth, who has Rodney's looks and Nora's spirit, loves twirling in the desert sun. Nora's content, though her mother's silence since before the wedding stings. She's never even met Elizabeth.

I spend the day reading, wrestling with the mysteries in the library books, especially that "tower." The answer feels close. I consider praying again, diving back into the Bible. It seems like life's only darkened without it.

When the day's over and night falls, I drift off, intent on talking to Cherie tomorrow. In my dream, a man is chasing me through the woods behind our house, a gun in his hand. I dodge, seeking cover, but he finds me. Just as he aims, about to fire, I wake, my eyes catching a giant shadow spider on the wall near my closet, watching me.

I pray for it to leave, and it slowly fades away. It reminds me of that thing I saw skittering on my window. I try to go back to sleep, and after a while I manage, waking to sunshine and birds. I dress for my riding lesson, still planning to go see Cherie before she heads to the mall with her friends.

I eat cereal for breakfast, though I'm not very hungry, and Mom and I drive to the stable soon after. I feel sad thinking about Cherie and how unhappy she's been recently.

Connie waves as we arrive. Mom and I wait on a bench by the entrance as she wraps up a group lesson. She chats with them a little, says goodbye, then turns to greet us. She asks if I'd like to go to a birthday party for one of the girls at the stable–Caroline–and I quickly agree. She smiles and says she'll give us directions after the lesson.

The lesson flies by, buoyed by the excitement of the party. Afterwards, Connie hands us a paper with the address. "Don't worry, you don't need to bring a gift," she says. "It's just a pizza and cake party."

"I'll bring candy," I say with a grin. She smiles at us, and we wave goodbye.

Back home, I decide to go for a walk, praying as I go. I plan to read the Bible later. I can feel the presence of God, supporting me, and I hope He'll guide my steps against these shadow entities. The hope lifts me.

The praying makes me feel better, and when I get back, I dive into the library books. Mom comes in and asks, "Have you been downstairs?"

"No," I reply. "Why?"

"I heard some kind of clicking noises. You know, like some sort of deep-throated language, like Swahili maybe."

"No," I say, "that wasn't me."

She seems a little distraught and begins to leave, then looks at me and says, "I saw more cigarette butts on the porch." With that, she turns and heads toward the stairs.

Cherie returns from the mall, later than expected, well past dinner. She heads upstairs to her room, and I steel myself to ask about Niffin. I feel the fear rising—what if she doubts me or hasn't seen what I have? Then I remember her wedding dress and ring, fleeting as they were. No, she's been touched by this too.

I knock on her cracked door. "Cherie? Can I come in?"

"I'm busy now. Let's talk tomorrow." I look through the opening and see a phone number on a piece of paper on her nightstand. She seems guarded, tied to it. I retreat, respecting her space.

I return to my room and the library books, Janis trailing behind. I hear Cherie walk down the stairs and pick up the kitchen phone. It sounds like she's talking with a boy—a boyfriend, maybe? Well that's it, mystery solved.

Reading lulls me to sleep. In my dream, I'm alone in a white shotgun house on a street filled with similar homes. A knock rattles the door, and I go to answer. Three men are standing there—one in tan, one in gray, one in blue—each in a double-breasted suit.

They want me to open the door, but I have a bad feeling. I stay still, hoping they'll leave. They don't, trying the locked door, then pounding and shaking it. I watch as they dart across the street, testing other homes with eerie, jerking speed—elbows high, unnatural.

The tan-suited man returns, prying against my lock forcefully. I brace the door, but he shoves through, breaching my space. I wake with a jolt, irritation lingering into the morning.

Downstairs, Cherie's at the breakfast nook. I ask if she's free. She puts me off again, suggesting the afternoon. Mom enters, reminding me of Caroline's party, and shows me a candy gift bag she got. She asks for the directions.

I search my room but can't find the paper. I spend all morning scouring for it, but I can't remember where it is. Mom grows increasingly restless as the hour of the party approaches. I barely know Caroline outside of the rides at the stable. She's nice enough, but it's not like we're close. Why all the fuss?

Time runs out. Mom's upset, calling me careless. I half-agree, puzzled. I've never lost papers before. Hours later, after the party, it hits me: the end table drawer by my recliner. Odd how it vanished from my mind, then snapped back like that.

I find Cherie in the library—finally, a chance to talk. I sit down and share what's on my mind. "Were you feeling sad when you were fishing at the dock?"

"Yes," she admits. "Well, more irritated, I guess." She tells me about a dream she had: three men in suits—tan, gray, and blue—tried breaking into her house, racing along the street with eerie speed. "One came back and forced his way through the door. I tried to hold it shut, but he broke through," she says with a shudder. "When he crashed in I woke up."

The shock hits me. Our dreams match, and it's the second time now. That woman I saw hovering over Mom, these shared visions—it's not a coincidence. My resolve hardens to solve this mystery.

"I'm glad it's nothing serious," I say to Cherie, returning to the book on my end table. She seems steady tonight. Maybe the dream shook her like it did me, and Mom's nagging about the directions just made it worse. We stay up late, Janis sleeps at my feet.

In the morning, I decide to rearrange my room. It's time for a change, and I set my old stuffed animals cheerily around my shoes in the closet. Mom looks in, clearly unimpressed. "Seems a little creepy," she says. I like it, so I decide to keep it like that for now.

"Did you ask Dad about me working at the store?"

"I did," she replies. "He's considering whether we need the extra help right now. I'll let you know what he decides."

I decide to take a walk, pray, and then come back and read the Bible. I'm feeling a little lighter. I ask Mom about church on Sunday, and to my delight she says we can go.

Today, she's driving me to return the library books, then taking Cherie and me for ice cream. We head to town, the warm, sunny day perfect. I watch the world roll by.

At the library, I drop off the books, looking for that helpful librarian, but she's nowhere to be seen. That's odd. I rejoin Mom and Cherie in the car.

The beach town is awash with tourists, slowing our drive to the ice cream shop. I don't mind though. I savor the outing, the radio, watching people shop and dine. Suddenly I think of Megan and Tony. I miss them, and those beach days with friends feel distant.

I order mint chocolate chip, but I don't see what Mom and Cherie get because I notice a blonde man across the street staring at me. He's handsome, with a blue shirt, plaid shorts, flip-flops, and blue sports car. There's a woman standing with him.

His gaze unnerves me. I pray and I get a quick, chilling answer: he wants me dead. Is it Niffin, masked again? I focus on my family and try to ignore him, but he keeps staring, and he doesn't vanish when I look away.

"What are you staring at?" Mom asks. "You've got ice cream dripping onto your shorts," she says in an exasperated tone. I wipe it off, eating as we leave. The man watches us go, then looks away as we climb into the station wagon.

That night, I hear my door lock click open and shut, and then footsteps, close. I face my dresser, frozen. The closet door creaks open, lingering. Those stuffed animals, is that what it's looking at? How would it know about them unless it's telepathic?

The door shuts, and the footsteps approach my bed. Something leaps, pinning me down. I can feel the weight, and I look up and see a human-sized shadow's on top of me. Panic rises in me—what now? The lamp's my best move. It sits still, knowing I'm alert. My heart pounding, I lunge, fumbling for the switch. The light blazes, and the shadow and the weight vanish. I get up and search under the bed, by the dresser, on the ceiling— nothing. How does it just dissolve like that? Shaken, I leave the lamp on and fall fitfully asleep.

In the morning, I bag the stuffed animals. I don't want the shadow to have a reason to come into my room ever again. I'll donate them. That thing felt human—leaping on top of me like that.

I head out for my customary walk, praying for God to banish the shadow. It's my new mission. I'll also check on the bees and boat with Dad and Cherie today because there has to be something normal in my life. But as I head for home, I can feel I'm being watched again. I hurry toward the house. When I reach the porch, I turn to see the crow with the blue-green eyes staring at me from a post on the boat dock.

CHAPTER 17

$\mathcal{N}$ora arrives home to find Rodney has returned earlier than expected. She rounds the corner to surprise him, but she freezes. There's a man with long dark hair standing there, startling her deeply. She slips back and calls out to Rodney. He responds quickly, assuring her he's there. She says nothing of the stranger, her eyes catching on a wooden box resting on the coffee table. When Rodney steps into the kitchen, a mix of impulse and uneasiness drives her to lift the lid. Inside, she finds bones, small bags of dirt, and jars of water—objects she recognizes as tools of witchcraft.

Her mother's words flood back, proven true in this moment. She closes the box swiftly, returning to her original spot, unaware that Rodney heard the faint click of the lid and knows she looked inside. She reflects on how rarely she prayed about marrying him, never seeking God's will. Regret settles heavily over her for allowing herself to make her choices without guidance.

Rodney reenters with a warm smile, offering her tea. She shakes her head, murmurs something about tending the garden, and moves to leave. His hand catches her arm as she passes, and she turns to face him, quaking at the anger flickering in his eyes.

Summer draws to a close once more, and this year I'll begin driver's ed. The thought of learning to drive excites me, promising a taste of independence. School starts soon, and I expect it to be productive, though likely solitary.

I've been praying for this year to improve, asking God to guide me through the challenges with the kids at school. Reading my Bible each day has brought a quiet strength back into my life.

Alone at home, I decide to make lunch. Janis barks sharply at the kitchen door. I get up to investigate. I peer through the window, seeing no one outside, and ensure the door is locked. As I return to my ham sandwich, her growling erupts again. I look out once more and catch sight of a tall figure ascending the steps—his skin stark white, his robe flowing, his face dominated by enormous black owl-like eyes above a small nose and mouth. He glares at me with a menace that chills my core.

Janis's barking breaks my focus for a moment; I glance at her, then back to the window—he's vanished. Doubt creeps in. Did I imagine him? As I return to my sandwich, a piece of paper on the island's edge flutters to the floor, as though brushed by someone rushing past. It couldn't be me; I'm standing too far away.

A growing unease settles over me. Janis stalks into the living room, barking fiercely, as if tracking something moving swiftly through the space. I can sense it now, a presence lingering in the house, heavy and unwelcome. I decide to get out of the house and walk in the neighborhood for a while. Once I can drive, escaping moments like these will be easier.

As I walk, I pray, asking God to lift the presence from our home. After an hour, I return to a quiet house—Janis is resting calmly, and the air feels clear. I wait for my parents to come back, and Cherie later in the afternoon.

As I lie in my bed that night, my thoughts turn to the upcoming school year and the beehives. Dad and I will need to ready them for winter by late September or early October. I take comfort in our three thriving hives this first year.

Soon, sleep takes me, and a dream unfolds. I'm walking toward an old desert church, its adobe walls painted white inside and out. A small entrance opens to a long hallway, with the sanctuary branching left. A modest wooden podium stands before an alcove, pews line the back, and a baptism pool sits to the right. Then the scene shifts—a modern school and city buildings swallow the church, erasing it from memory. Like my other dreams, I can feel the weight of someone else's longing and sorrow, though I don't know whose.

I wake in the dark, rolling over to chase more sleep. Morning finally arrives, and I'm blanketed with a deep depression. I can't bring myself to pray or open my Bible, blocked by some unseen force. I know I'm still cursed.

I give in, letting the dark oppression steer me away from devotion, filling my day with other tasks instead. My parents take us to church, but the sermon slips past me. I can't focus, no matter how hard I try, and I can't figure out why. Tomorrow marks the first day back at my old school—I'm transferring back. I'm nervous and annoyed. I wish school would just be over already so I can move on to a job or college.

My alarm blares, and for a moment, I forget it's the first day of school. Memory quickly dawns, and I groan, rising reluctantly to dress. The days of careful back-to-school shopping, once brimming with hope, feel distant now. I miss that lightness.

Mom drives me to school, and I head to the first class listed on my orientation schedule. The day unfolds quietly. I chat with a few girls from last year, settling into new routines and classes.

Driver's ed is my final class, the only one I truly anticipate. As I walk to the auditorium, a tall, cute guy with dark hair, tan skin, and striking blue eyes comes up to me and engages me in small talk. I'm pleasantly surprised when he's assigned the seat next to mine.

The first week slips by, and I feel a little lighter. I return to praying after school and reading my Bible in the evenings. My life is reduced to a simple rhythm—hobbies, schoolwork, and casual acquaintances rather than deep friendships.

By the second week, sitting next to that cute boy—Owen—makes my hands sweat and my heart race. His blue eyes gleam like fine topaz, and I realize I'm smitten. Sitting beside him, I feel as though I could drift away, but my feelings are invisible to him and everyone else.

Then, without warning, the depression crashes in again, unbidden, discouraging my prayers and Bible reading. I see the pattern now—stopping, restarting—and I sense the shadow meddling, assaulting me with its telepathic energy, posing as God to derail me. Strange thoughts begin to run through my head: I'm a witch, wielding wondrous powers, like telekinesis and levitation. They come and go, tantalizing yet fleeting.

I stop praying again, waiting for the heaviness to lift. My curiosity about magic is growing, though I never pursue it.

I catch glimpses of Owen around school. He's popular, refined, and I can smell his salon gel whenever I'm close. He's flawless in an effortless way. I lack the confidence to talk to him or his friends.

The weekend dawns, and I'm eager for my riding lesson. I finish up some homework and study during the day. Later, when evening comes, I decide to read downstairs in the living room while my family's upstairs. The change is kind of nice, but the Victorian couch is not as cozy as my recliner.

Fatigue nudges me toward bed. As I reach the foyer, I see a tall man pivoting toward the stairs. He spots me on the couch. His robe and face are pitch black, split by a red stripe down the center. He glares at me with owl eyes, his small features twisted in anger and long hair faintly visible.

I'm frozen by his hostile stare. Should I run? Scream? Janis bounds in, barking loudly, pulling my gaze. When I look back, the man's gone, just like before.

I climb upstairs with Janis, sleeping with the lamp on. The image of that man haunts me, but prayer soothes me enough to fall sleep. Janis stays with me all night, keeping watch. In the morning, I insist on going to church. Mom's weary from yesterday, but she agrees, and I feel restored after the service.

On Monday, we practice driving at school. There's a separate parking lot set up with cones and cars. Owen's waiting on a bench for his turn. I can't keep my eyes off of him, but I can't muster the nerve to speak. How I wish I could—even if he doesn't like me, at least I'll know.

At home, I ask Mom if we can go out driving to practice.

"Sure," she agrees. We get in the care, and I ease down our neighborhood road. She tenses up as I get too close to the mailboxes. It's all so new, and the car feels so big on these narrow lanes. I do my best to adjust, keeping the car steady.

"Why don't you drive us to the mall," she suggests, sounding braver than I'm sure she's feeling. "Or maybe ice cream?"

"Which way's less crowded?" I ask.

"Probably ice cream, since it's not tourist season anymore."

On the way, Mom points out every flaw in my driving, clutching the handle like a life raft. Her reactions don't bother me all that much. I know I'll get better, and driving around like this makes me feel independent. Mom brings up Caroline's party and reminds me to leave the candy I promised with Connie at my next lesson.

My parking at the shop is not the best. Mom's constant criticism isn't helping, that's for sure, and I wonder if maybe that's why I lack confidence. I mean, she knows it's the first time I'm driving outside of class.

We go inside and decide to try the new cherry vanilla ice cream. It's rich and delightful. She treats us to two scoops. "Good job getting us here in one piece," she says. I note the change in tone, but I am pretty proud of myself.

We stroll the beach strip, cones in hand, window-shopping. Mom lingers over white sandals with silver bead flowers. I'm a little surprised by the choice, but she admires them awhile before we move on. Seagulls circle overhead, eyeing our ice cream and diving close in hopes we'll drop some.

Once finished, we start home. I feel that prickly sensation of being watched again. It's rare beyond the house. I scan the road, but I can't see anyone or anything looking at me. Then a wad of newspaper, soaked with what looks like soup, slaps across the windshield, obscuring everything. I ease off the gas, flicking on the wipers and spraying fluid to clear it. Praying softly, I lower my window so I can see ahead as the mess shifts around the windshield.

"Pull over!" Mom yells, panic in her voice, but the moment's passed. The wipers sweep the last of it away, and we're unharmed. As we continue on, Mom lectures me about what I should have done, but my mind strays to *how* it happened. That paper fell straight down, like someone dropped it from right over the car, and there was no one beside us when it happened.

We reach the driveway and inspect the car—no damage, just streaks of residue. I fetch a bucket and hose, washing it clean as Mom watches briefly before heading inside.

That feeling of being watched creeps back over me. I hear a caw and turn to see the familiar crow with bluish-green eyes perched on the garage roof, staring at me intently.

CHAPTER 18

*N*ora quietly ushers Elizabeth into the train station, their belongings bundled close. She is going to stay with her father's family in Tennessee, a break from Rodney's shadow. As the train rumbles forward, she peers out the window and spots a wolf running parallel to the tracks. Its bluish-green eyes shimmer in the fading light, and she stares at it uneasily.

The wolf soon fades from sight, allowing Nora to exhale in quiet relief. The train whistle blasts, jolting her upright. Her nerves, frayed from the escape, betray her outward calm.

Christmas is approaching swiftly. Nora shifts in her aisle seat, waiting for Elizabeth to return from chatting with a child a few rows back. She hears Elizabeth call "Dad!" before the girl dashes toward the back of the train. Nora leaps up and pursues her, but in under thirty seconds, Elizabeth disappears—impossible for a small child on a sealed train.

Nora combs the cars tirelessly, aided by confused strangers. Denial battles disbelief as she glances out the window once more. The wolf returns, now with a cub at its side, loping beside the train. Realization crashes over her: The wolf is Rodney, and he has claimed Elizabeth. Grief and guilt wash over her. She weeps without restraint, blaming herself for everything.

Christmas is getting closer. Excitement stirs as Mom decorates the living room and entrance with red and green hues. Wreaths, poinsettias, and snowman pillows brighten the couches. Soon we'll go pick out a live tree at a nearby lot, a yearly family ritual. There's so much to look forward to. This spring, Cherie and Owen will graduate high school, and this summer, we're going on a cruise.

Janis growls at a strand of garland peeking from a decoration box. I laugh as she sniffs it, trying to look inside. Her stiffness hints at arthritis, slowing her once-lively stride.

"Well, what do you want for Christmas?" Mom asks me. I tell her I'll think it over. To be honest, I'm not really sure, though I do wish Janis could be a puppy again.

Mom's eager to visit the tree lot today, and Dad agrees. Still no word on working at the store, and I don't understand why I can't get an answer.

The air is cold and biting, so I don my coat, boots, and jeans. On the drive, I think about possible gifts while Cherie sits quietly, her thoughts elsewhere. I'm more excited about the summer cruise to Mexico, even if it's only for a day.

"We should go to the mall tomorrow for some Christmas shopping," says Mom. I nod with a smile. This is her season, and we humor her, even if it doesn't make a lot of sense to us. Thoughts of school and Owen drift into my mind too. I'll miss him next year. He's dating Mandy now, her beauty and popularity a mirror to his own.

Dad pulls into the tree lot, and we fan out to find the ideal tree. I wander to the back where it's quieter and spot a good one—wide at the base, narrowing toward the top. I call Mom over, and she inspects it carefully, spinning it every which way. She approves but insists on browsing more. "Hold onto it while I look around," she commands.

After a bit, she returns with a smile. "You found the best one!"

Dad pays, and we load it into our station wagon. The scent of fresh pine fills the car as we head home.

When we get back, Dad and I wrestle the tree into its stand, nestling it between the left and back walls. Mom dives into decorating with gusto, and I step away for a moment. I look over at Janis napping in the kitchen; she sleeps more these days. After a little break, I rejoin them. Mom and Dad are singing carols and have the lights strung already.

The rest of the year races to an end. Tonight marks Cherie's graduation. She wears a blue formal dress beneath her blue-and-gold cap and gown. Once Mom's ready, we load up the car and head off to the ceremony.

Cherie sits among the graduates, all in orderly rows. We settle into bleacher seats and wait. I excuse myself for the bathroom; on my way back, someone nearly collides with me. It's Owen. He pauses to greet me and share his summer plans. The loudspeaker signals the start of the ceremony. "See you later," he says.

"Sure, you too." I echo the sentiment, but inside I have my doubts. His departure is looming, and this casual goodbye cuts me pretty deep.

A month passes, and the cruise is only a week away. I pack my suitcase carefully with clothes and essentials. Mom suggests getting me a new sunhat and sandals. I toss in a sundress and cute shorts for the four-day jaunt to Mexico and the Florida Keys.

I think about her offer, tempted to drive to the beach strip for them. Owen flickers in my mind—where is he now? I try to shake the thought from my head and focus on the days ahead instead.

Before we go, the beehives will need extra attention. Guess I'll skip riding lessons for a couple weeks. Maybe a little change in routine is a good thing anyway, helping to take my mind off of all the bad things happening in my life.

Mom okays a shopping trip for cruise gear. I drive us, window down for fresh air. At the strip, I choose a navy blue sunhat and off-white sandals. She buys them and picks a pair of brown floral ones for herself.

The drive home is filled with glowing sunlight and a soft breeze. I park in the garage and smile. At least Mom's not criticizing my driving anymore.

Upstairs, I set my new items by the suitcase. I walk back downstairs and find Janis sleeping in her bed. Her arthritis keeps her from coming up the stairs. I feel her absence keenly; she's been my steady companion when others have let me down.

The week hums by as I help Mom clean and furnish Cherie's dorm room. I love her mini fridge the most. She also has a new pink-and-purple quilt, floral bedding, office supplies, and a pink beanbag, all compliments of Mom.

Cherie seems to be pretty happy about the college experience so far, but I miss her and wish that things could stay like they were for a while longer. I'm not ready for the next chapter of life because I never really got to live my current one.

Well, at least she's joining us on the cruise. Mom picks her up from the dorm, and she stays at house overnight before we head to Florida. Janis is staying with Aunt Rosalyn while we're away.

I wake in the morning to my parents bustling in the kitchen, buzzing with nervousness about the trip. I crave peace on vacation, but it's not easy with those two. Mom makes us pancakes while Dad loads the car. Cherie shuffles in, half-awake with rollers in hair, grabbing a cup of coffee.

We plan the trip over breakfast. Dad has the stops all mapped out, with the lunch spots picked by Mom. Cherie seems a little tense, then suddenly blurts out, "I'm getting married!"

Mom and Dad just stare, stunned. "When did you even start dating?" I ask, suddenly remembering that phone number on the nightstand and Cherie's private call in the kitchen. Mom looks tense and says we'll talk about it after the trip.

We pile into the car for the twelve-hour drive. It's sunny and warm, growing ever hotter as we get closer to Florida. We finally arrive in Tampa, and find our hotel. It's clean, and it has a pool—sparking cheers from Cherie and me. Mom grins. "Go on, swim," she says. The warm water is soothing. I float, thinking about Janis and teasing Cherie about her boyfriend.

That night, I nudge the curtain open for a little bit of light. I drift into sleep but wake up in the middle of the night to a human-sized shadow at the window. When it sees that I'm awake it shifts back and forth, pacing like it doesn't know what to do, and then it's gone. I debate closing the curtains but decide to leave it until morning, drifting back to sleep.

We board the cruise ship via a long gangplank into a bustling check-in hall. A vivid hallway with elevators follows. "Look, Mom," I tease, "your sandals match the carpet." She chuckles and we make our way to our room.

It's got an ocean view room, a balcony, two beds, and a fold-out couch.

The wide window and glass door promise refuge from the crowded decks. It'll be a wonderful place to relax and enjoy the cruise.

Cherie and I explore and find a track with a bunch of exercise equipment facing vast floor-to-ceiling windows. Mom calls us to the bow as the ship sails. People on the shore folks wave, and we wave in reply as the horn sounds, the giant ship gliding out to sea.

After roaming around the ship, we head to the dining room for the formal meal. It's elegant with white tablecloths and wine for adults. I order lobster for the first time, but it's bland.

Dawn brings the Florida Keys. We debark and tour downtown in a van. It's small, colonial, floral, and wonderfully calm. Afterward, we put on gear and go snorkeling. The blue waters are brimming with curious fish. I graze a massive coral reef, awed by its scale and the risk it presents to ships.

The next day, we visit the Mayan ruins at Tulum. The water shifts from turquoise to topaz, breathtakingly vivid. A tram through the jungle takes us to the beachside site. There's no tour, just plaques to guide us. The temple looms grand but distant. A sheltered altar grabs my attention. We're not supposed to go in, but I'm intrigued. Suddenly, a shadow surges forward, pushing me into the stone and cutting my shin. Luckily, Mom has a Band-Aid.

I'm shocked though. How could this happen in broad daylight? I feel that sensation of being watched, and it stays with me through Tulum and Carmen del Playa, not leaving me in peace until we board the ship again.

After taking a shower, I re-bandage my leg and step out onto the balcony alone. I pray to God to take away this shadow and whatever it is that's stopping me from praying consistently. It's so peaceful and beautiful here in Mexico. Bible in hand, I rejoin my family for Mom's beloved formal dinner.

CHAPTER 19

Two years after escaping, Nora's working as a nurse and has met a new man: Arthur. She calls herself Beatrice now, shielding her past. While no one presses her about it, the loss of Elizabeth festers within her, a quiet ache she'll bear to her end, something that no one in her new life will ever know.

A package arrives one day: a portrait of a ballerina. She knows it's Elizabeth, and though it wounds her deeply, she keeps it, hanging it on the wall near her bedroom. She looks at it and smiles each day, holding tight to the memory of the child she loved and imagining the woman she became.

She marries Arthur, raising three children together. Still, Rodney and Elizabeth linger in her heart. Rodney alone eased her solitude. Red roses and white lilies grace her home, a secret tribute that Arthur mistakes for mere taste.

Back from the cruise, I unpack, musing on my last school year without Cherie or Owen. I'll likely keep to myself a lot, hoping time hurries past.

I place my new sandals in the closet, smiling at my memories of the cruise. A thud behind the wall stops me cold. I hear footsteps ascending stairs. I need to find Mom and ask her some questions about our house.

Mom's downstairs in the kitchen, cooking with Janis lying nearby. I settle at the breakfast nook. "Have you unpacked?e" she asks.

"Not yet. Mom," I ask, shifting the subject, "why's the library window covered up like that?"

She agrees it's odd. "Maybe it was cheaper than renovating an old house," she suggests. "After Great-Grandma died, Granddad fled the house, swearing it was haunted by a ballerina. Of course, everyone just brushed it off, saying he was seeing things.

The house stayed vacant for a while until my Aunt Susie inherited it. Everyone always wondered why Arthur never sold but made a condition in his will that it had to stay in the family. According to Susie, this is how the house was when she found it. I guess some things are just mysteries."

I resolve to check that wall tomorrow when Mom and Dad are at the store. Cherie's fiancé is joining us Friday, so it's my window of opportunity.

I go for a walk and pray, then read my Bible when I get back. I continue pleading for God to remove whatever it is that's blocking my faith. While my mood swings have softened, there's still some force fighting my prayers —but I persist.

I sleep, eager for what I'll discover tomorrow. I dream Janis has passed away. I wake in the middle of the night, feeling as if I'm being held by two sets of arms, one on my lower back. Unsure whether it's real or a dream, I push the feeling aside and try to get back to sleep.

Morning proves the dream real. I find Janis, still and unmoving in her bed. I call Mom, tears streaming down my face. I cradle her in my arms, telling her to sleep well and to play fetch in the fields of Heaven.

Mom gets a box, and we place her inside with her toys and her blanket. It's a somber moment as I say goodbye to my truest friend.

We get a bouquet of flowers for her funeral. I weep as we dig a hole, lay her box inside, and cover her with dirt. I set the flowers on top. Her death leaves a hole that no one can fill.

Mom leaves to join Dad at the store. I head inside, resolved to figure out what's going on in the closet. I clear away shoes and clothes and run my hands over the back wall. It feels flimsy; strange for a remodel. I press, and it shifts, more like a prop than a real wall. Is there a secret passage?

I push and a crack opens enough to let me peer through. Light spills from an open window—closed outside—and I see stairs climbing upward. I push it open further and squeeze in. I consider taking the time to grab a weapon, but curiosity drives me up the stairs.

A familiar creak echoes as I ascend. Off-white walls, untouched since sealed, frame maple stairs that are nothing like the oak stairs in the rest of the house. A musty scent hangs in the air.

At the landing, an open, screenless window glows. To the right, there's a large room that's empty except for a stone altar like the one at Tulum, carved with faint, ancient markings.

My amethyst ring is sitting there, along with Mom's gold earrings, Cherie's silver bracelet, and Dad's pocket watch—all lost treasures. There are some unfamiliar items too: an old hairpin, antique jewelry, a silver angel necklace. Maybe things from past kin?

All of these things have one thing in common: They're our dearest possessions, turned against us. There are strange words written on papers in a language I don't recognize. Ash and layered powders dust the stone. An incense stick juts from the wall, smoldering recklessly.

I see a folding table against the back wall, bearing our photos, messages scrawled on the back in that same script. I can feel the dread rising in me. What's going on, and who's doing this?

I grab the items and photos, pluck the incense from the wall, and take it and hurl it into the river outside. I return to lock the window and rinse the powder off the altar.

Uncertain of what to do with all the things I found, I fetch a ceramic planter, pile in newspaper along with the items and photos, and burn everything in the driveway. I watch the flames. Even the jewelry melts—well, at least some of it— and I keep adding paper until everything burns. I dump the ashes in the lake.

Afterward, I grab a sledgehammer from the garage and shatter the altar to rubble, hauling it and the table down to the lake and dumping it too.

Weary yet proud, I fix myself a sandwich with chips. Back in the room, I pray, asking God to bind any evil spirits and cleanse the family of witchcraft, demons, and shadows. I leave an old Bible where the altar stood. I'm sure whatever it was will return through that window, and it'll be furious.

I sleep with the lamp on, wondering whether I can ask Mom to switch to

Cherie's room since she's not here anymore. I wake to the sound of a whiny girl's voice calling my name from the closet wall. She repeats a few times, and then I hear knocking. Is something going to come for me? I shout for it to leave in Jesus's name over and over.

The knocking stops, but I can hear footsteps roaming the hallway. Fearing that there might be another entrance, I switch the light on in the hall—it's empty. I screw up my courage and check downstairs. I hear whispering in the dining room. The French doors are shut, but I can see three figures pacing, one shorter than the others, calling me in that little girl voice. I stand frozen for a moment and then pray out loud again, invoking the name of Jesus to make them leave. They grow quiet and slowly fade away.

I rush upstairs and barricade myself in Cherie's room, pulling her dresser against the door. When I finally fall asleep, the light's are still on. Somehow, my parents sleep through it all.

In my dream, I'm at my pastor's house. I'm talking to his wife and son, but they just ignore me. The pastor's wife asks to speak with me privately. She pulls me aside, locking us in a room. She strikes me hard, advancing as I retreat, her gaze full of menace. "You think you can leave us?" she snarls. It snaps me awake.

I see a shadow spider looming in the corner; it fades when it notices me watching. I pray for God to make these entities leave me alone. I fall asleep beside the bed.

In the morning, I pull the dresser aside and go to check out my room. The window's open—they came last night. I close it, pray again, and leave, hoping God ends this horror soon.

CHAPTER 20

*R*odney settles into an opulent dining chair at a wide, pristine table. He sits quietly, lost in thoughts of everything that has happened with Nora. His brother Niffin notices the sadness clouding his expression and asks if she's the cause of his mood. Rodney brushes it off at first, claiming things are fine now that he has Elizabeth.

Niffin locks eyes with him and suggests a chilling plan. He tells Rodney to place a generational curse on Nora and her descendants, arguing that they have no right to exist since she should only have children with Rodney. He says they should destroy her family line with Arthur completely, erasing what never should have taken root. Rodney finds the notion appealing, and together they conjure a powerful curse to bind her lineage.

I struggle with the idea of telling Mom and Dad about the secret room upstairs, unsure if I should mention it at all. They own this house, yet they've never bothered to investigate the wall covering the library window. Their refusal to look deeper feels like a choice to ignore whatever might be lurking in our home.

Tonight, Cherie is bringing her fiancé over for dinner. I feel a flutter of nerves about meeting him, though I can tell Cherie's anxiety runs even deeper. Knowing that Mom's preparing shepherd's pie lifts my spirits a little.

I take my morning prayer walk and spend time with my Bible afterward. The mood swings that used to plague me have softened, though I still find it hard to pray consistently. I keep at it, trying to let go of willing sin and asking God to shape my life according to His will.

Cherie arrives home looking radiant in a red spaghetti-strap dress adorned with navy blue embroidered flowers. Her hair is swept into a messy bun, held together by navy flower clips, and her face is glowing with red lips, a touch of blush, and blue eyeshadow. I admire her navy sandals, their floral stitching a perfect match for her outfit.

Her fiancé walks in wearing a black suit paired with a light purple shirt, which makes me smile quietly to myself. He's tall, with dusty blonde hair and pale blue eyes, and something about him feels familiar—maybe from school or the beach. I'm sure I'll figure it out soon. The feeling of faint recognition keeps tugging at me.

We move into the dining room and chat lightly while waiting for dinner to finish cooking. Dad is most eager for conversation, while I sit there, my hunger growing with every whiff of shepherd's pie drifting from the kitchen.

It turns out that Ryan, Cherie's fiancé, went to our high school and used to hang out with Owen. "Owen? How's he doing," I ask.

"He's doing well," he replies. The news stirs a hollow ache inside me, but I hide it well enough that no one notices my expression falter.

Mom carries in the shepherd's pie and places it on a hot pad in the center of the table. Dad says grace, and we start eating. A wave of sadness washes over me as they talk and laugh, so I excuse myself and go into the kitchen. I glance at the spot where Janis's bed used to be, imagining her nudging my feet for scraps tonight.

As I rest against the island, the phone rings. "Hello?" There's no response. "Hello," I say again. There's still no response, so I hang up. This is the first one of those silent calls in a long time. I take a few minutes to gather myself before heading back into the dining room. After dinner, we play Monopoly with Ryan, and Dad jokes that he's testing Ryan's financial sense, though I know he's not entirely kidding.

Ryan heads home, and Cherie stays behind. "Well, what do you think of him," she asks excitedly.

"He seems like a nice young man," says Mom. "And grandkids would be a blessing, seeing as our family hasn't had many lately." She laughs at our expressions and says, "Well, someone needs to keep this family going."

Her comment makes me pause. Our line does seem to be thinning out. I think back to those photos from the secret room—pictures of us and other relatives with unfamiliar writing on the back. Could infertility be part of the curse?

I don't really know how far the curse stretches, but I resolve to keep praying and growing closer to God. That's my only defense against these shadow entities. The ballerina portrait bothers me—it must be cursed too. I doubt my parents would get rid of it though, so I just pray over it every day during when I head out the door for my walks.

Time moves on, and my senior year of high school passes quickly, mostly uneventful and solitary. I miss seeing Cherie and Owen in the hallways; even my old dreams of them feel distant now. Janis's absence makes the house feel emptier than ever.

I still go to horseback riding lessons, though I've reached a turning point. I know enough to have my own horse someday, but it won't happen here at my parents' place. When I move out and start my own life, I'll finally get my own horse, and the thought brings a smile to my face.

I rarely visit the library anymore, buried under homework this last year of high school. It's a fair trade, I guess, since it's the final stretch of assignments they'll ever get to throw at me.

My parents and I go to church on Sundays and now Wednesday nights as well. Spiritually, I feel lighter these days, and I sense a miracle might be coming soon, even if I can't guess what it'll be.

On Friday, Ryan and Cherie come over for dinner again. As he greets us, he mentions a cool neighbor who owns a black two-door Dodge Charger parked nearby.

"What are you talking about?" I ask pointedly.

He shrugs. "It probably belongs to someone in the area."

At school, I hear my friends talking about getting into colleges and universities or receiving application offers. It gets me thinking about what I want. I remember how much I loved building theater sets. I start researching film schools and apply to a few without telling anyone.

On Saturday, I borrow the station wagon to drive to the beach for lunch while Mom and Dad are at work. The day is sunny and pleasantly cool, so I park and eat at the restaurant Megan and I used to love back when I still had a best friend. I miss those times, though Niffin's tricks have shown me how unreliable people can be. Now I know God's the only one I can truly count on.

After eating, I walk along the beach, and my thoughts turn to Tony. I wonder what he's up to these days and how his life's going. Even though it feels like we never really knew each other, I still miss him a little, just like Megan, though it's starting to fade.

As I head back to the car, a black 1969 two-door Dodge Charger drives by and honks. A shadowy figure waves from the driver's seat, sending a shiver through me. I hurry to the station wagon, eager to get home.

On the drive back, I spot the Charger in my rearview mirror, speeding up and honking as it closes in. It swerves to pass me, nearly brushing my front headlight, then races ahead. When I reach the curve and the road straightens, it's gone. Where did it go? I remind myself to pray every time I get behind the wheel, especially with these shadow entities around.

When I pull into the driveway, I see that car parked across the street. It could be a different one. I mean, it's not a common model, but it's possible. I go inside and start praying, asking God for protection.

I spend a long time in prayer, then look around my room, noticing a few dirty clothes that need to go in the hamper and some dust on the furniture. I mentally list the chores I should tackle soon.

I hear footsteps approaching my bedroom door. When I turn, there's a human-sized shadow standing right beside me, close enough that our shoulders nearly touch. I remember the face: dark owl-like eyes, a small nose, and a tiny mouth. It smiles and glances around my room, taking in the scattered clothes and dusty surfaces as if passing judgment. I feel a flash of irritation at this thing invading my space and sizing it up like that.

The shadow looks back at me, still smiling, almost cheerful. I start to wonder if I'm really seeing this, but I keep my eyes on it, not daring to reach out and check if it's solid.

I look closer and notice it has two sets of arms: one pair at the shoulders like mine, and another just above its waist. I stare at that second set, caught between amazement and unease.

When I glance back up at its face, the shadow's eyes are burning with anger, growing fiercer by the second until they're blazing with rage. Panic overwhelms me, and I run out of the room, grabbing my purse and keys. I jump into the station wagon and drive off, praying as I go with no clear destination in mind.

After driving aimlessly for a while, I head back home and pray some more before settling down with my Bible. Mom and Dad come home later, but I don't tell them what happened.

A few days later, a letter arrives from Arizona, which strikes me as odd since I don't know anyone there. I open it expecting junk mail, but it's an acceptance letter to a film school called Diamond Filled Purple Night Skies Productions. I didn't apply to it, but I tuck it away, figuring it might be useful if the local college falls through.

May rolls around, and it's my turn to graduate in a cap and gown. Cherie, Ryan, Mom, and Dad show up, but my thoughts drift to Niffin and what lies ahead. We go out for pizza afterward, and Cherie asks, "What are you planning to do next?"

"I applied to the local college," I reply.

She looks a bit let down. "I always imagined you'd head off to London or somewhere exciting after high school." I just stare at my pizza and stay quiet for the rest of the night.

Mom and Dad decide it's time for Mom to get a new car, which means I'll inherit the station wagon. Of course, she's excited at the thought of me staying nearby for college, but deep down it feels wrong—I'm tired of living up to what they expect. Maybe Cherie's right, maybe I do want something bold and adventurous after all.

Another letter comes, this time from the local college, confirming my acceptance. I show it to Mom and call to set up the orientation, though I can't stop thinking about that mysterious Arizona school and how I got accepted without applying.

At the orientation, they can't find my student number, so I go to the registrar's office with Mom. The receptionist is brusque and hands me a number to call a supervisor. The next day, the supervisor tells me I need to pay another application fee and send my high school transcripts again, even though I already did both. She says the extra fee will be refunded once it's processed, but I don't buy it—it feels like they've lost my stuff or given my spot to someone else.

I arrange a date to drop off the new transcripts and fee, then head upstairs to pull out the Arizona letter again. I dial the number on it, and a woman answers. Too nervous to admit I didn't apply, I ask about the fall class. She explains how to sign up for a dorm and register for courses.

I decide to check if the school's legitimate, so I head to the library and call the Arizona Department of Education to confirm its accreditation. They say it's a real school, which leaves me stunned and intrigued.

The next morning, while Mom's making tea in the kitchen, I sit at the breakfast nook and ask what she thinks about Arizona.

"Arizona? It's too far away to even think about," she says.

"I'm going there for film school," I blurt out.

Her teacup slips from her hand and shatters on the floor. She stares at me, her face tight. "What?"

I sit with her and explain why I think it's the right choice, especially with the hassle from the local college. That night, we talk it over with Dad, and he takes it much better than expected, even offering $2,500 to help me get started out west. It's all starting to feel real—a new chapter waiting for me.

CHAPTER 21

*E*verything is set with the film school now that I've registered for classes and secured a dorm room. Mom insists on driving with me to Arizona, though I feel confident handling it alone. Since Dad gave me the money for the trip and she plans to fly back after settling me in, I agree to let her come along.

I spend the summer packing here and there while looking up fun things to do in Arizona, like visiting the Grand Canyon. As August nears, my excitement builds steadily. Mom suggests a beach trip and lunch soon, as well as an end-of-summer party to send me off with friends and family.

I settle on holding the farewell party in a few weeks. Today, Mom wants to hash out the details over pizza at a beachside restaurant. I drive us there, feeling a bittersweet tug—sadness at leaving this town mixes with relief, as I've grown so detached from it over time. Passing places tied to lost friends like Megan and Tony stings, and I wonder again why those bonds faded. I miss them keenly in that fleeting moment of memory.

We pull up to the restaurant and step into a cozy dining room with red faux-leather chairs and a red-and-white checkered tile floor. A soda fountain with stools lines the left wall. We order sodas served in tall, tinted red plastic cups filled with crushed ice. As I sip mine and glance around, recalling bits of this town, Mom tells me about the party she's planning at home—a small gathering with ice cream cake and her famous punch. She's always looking for a reason to whip up that recipe.

The day before the party, Mom passes my room and asks, "Why were you up so late last night?"

I give her a puzzled look. "I wasn't," I reply.

"But I heard you rummaging around in your room after 2 a.m. There was a light under your door," she insisted, "and I even heard some whispering."

A queasy feeling hits me—I act in a hurry to pack so my mom leaves, and I don't have to explain anything to her. I spend the day finishing my packing and hauling stuff to the car. It's a bigger job than I'd expected, lugging it all down the kitchen stairs and out front. Waiting a day to leave after this feels smart; I'll need the rest before the long drive. I imagine Janis trailing me out here if she were still alive, and I miss the neighborhood kids who used to visit. Lately, I feel disconnected from this place and even from God, with no clue why.

The evening of the party arrives. I keep thinking about how distant I've grown from God. Mom sets up in the dining room: punch bowl and glasses on the left, chocolate ice cream cake and brownies on the right with plates, napkins, and spoons. I help arrange it all, and the guests start trickling in—Cherie and Ryan first, then Uncle Tom, Mom's brother, followed by a few school acquaintances. No neighbors show, which doesn't surprise me. Mom only told a couple she knows, and I've lost touch with everyone else here.

I spot Cherie and Ryan scooping up some ice cream cake. She murmurs to him, faintly audible, that she's shocked I'm off to film school since I never cared for it before and that I'm clearly the favorite with our parents footing my tuition, dorm, travel, and just giving me their old car. Her words sting— I'm annoyed, knowing they're bankrolling her lavish wedding and a house down payment.

I duck into the kitchen to escape them for a moment, grabbing more brownies and a platter for the table. Later, Mom wants to open the few graduation gifts I got. As I pile brownies onto one of her crystal plates, the grandfather clock at the top of the stairs chimes. I turn to admire it—I've always loved that clock—when Uncle Tom startles me, appearing behind me with a bitter tone, saying he was supposed to inherit it. I glance back at the clock, then at him again, but he's gone. Moments later, I see him in the dining room chatting with Cherie and Ryan as if nothing happened. I open the gifts, thanking everyone: a coffee mug with a diploma and "congratulations," a class ring from my parents, a few cards with twenty-dollar bills, and a small box wrapped in white fabric with a pink mesh bow. Inside sits a gold locket.

"Is this some sort of joke?" she demands, picking it up with a frown. "That's the locket my dad gave me, passed to me before I was even born. It was lost years ago—and my mother always blamed me..." She trails off, checking for a note, but there's none.

Things quickly become awkward, and the mood of the party changes. The guests start to filter out, leaving just Dad, Mom, and me. I help Dad clean up while Mom stares at the locket, visibly upset. She's fixating on how it got lost and the fallout, not the eerie fact that it reappeared at my party. I gather my gifts, stow them in the car, and head to bed early.

I don't ask Mom when she wants to leave tomorrow—she's still riled about the locket. She can't go without me, so I'll set the pace. Lying there, I feel sad, regretting that I didn't pray for the party to go well. I've slacked on prayer and Bible reading lately; a heavy energy drags me down whenever I try, leaving me discouraged.

I try to sleep, but my mind drifts to the secret room. Is the window open again, or are there more surprises like the locket up there? On my last night here for a while, I decide to check. I grab a flashlight, open the secret door, and climb the steps. I feel bold at first, but a rustling stops me. I aim the light at the top of the stairs where I heard the sound—nothing's there. I turn to leave and head back to bed.

Mom's knock wakes me in the morning. She's eager to get me up and moving. I dress, pack my nightgown next to my purse, eat a bowl of cereal, grab my toiletries, and head to the car. As I head through the front door, I look back at the house wistfully, the place I've lived in all my life. I feel a pang of loss, but I'm glad for a fresh start, hoping to find my own home soon.

Mom approaches the passenger side, her purse stuffed with maps she and Dad have pored over. I've never been out west, so I'm curious what awaits—lots of desert beauty, I hope. She climbs in, setting her purse by her left leg, clearly as thrilled as I am for the trip. Dad waves from the driveway. I wave back and pull out of the driveway, emotions swirling as we leave the subdivision. I feel relief and joy for what's ahead, but sorrow for the friendships left behind.

Ten minutes in, Mom wants diet sodas from a machine. I stop at a shopping plaza, we grab drinks, and then we head off toward the interstate. The green foliage and bright blue sky feel like good omens for the journey.

A few hours later, I take an exit to refuel and get more drinks. Mom heads inside for beverages while I pump the gas. She offers to pay for it all at the counter, and soon we're back on the road. Traffic thickens heading west, and my nerves jangle. I'm not as experienced on the interstate as the other drivers around me.

We cross two states today before stopping for the night, picking an exit with affordable hotels. We choose a white-painted brick one with a Spanish flair. Mom pays inside while I wait under the porte-cochère, then I drive us around to a first-floor room. It's cool and clean, with double beds draped in jungle-plant comforters—no animals—and thick hunter-green blackout curtains over sheer white ones.

I claim the bed by the window, a habit, and sink into it, exhausted. I dream of Mom and me trekking through a field of dry grass, reddish-brown dirt peeking through sparse patches. We reach Native American cliff dwellings, too far to explore without a guide. We gaze at them until a dirt road emerges, cars rolling toward a ticket office, gift shop, and restaurant. Mom, parched from the desert walk, heads there for a diet soda to rest.

I wake with an odd feeling, as if I knew those dwellings and their people, now lost. I make a note to check later whether Navajo had cliff dwellings like in my dream. Mom rises, keen for the hotel breakfast. I dress slowly in the bathroom as she waits.

We head to the dining room near the lobby. A green counter along a tan wall holds cereal, a fruit bowl with oranges and bananas, toast with butter and jam, instant oatmeal, and bagels with cream cheese. Mom, clearly underwhelmed, grabs some tea and toast. I see milk, orange juice, and a hot water tap next to a coffee maker with tea bags. I opt for cereal, milk, and juice. Mom grabs bananas and offers me a bagel. She's eager to hit the road hard today.

We check out and drive on. Time rolls by, and the trees shrink as we reach Alabama. Mom suggests stopping for lunch and a checking the map.

At a local diner, I get that feeling of being watched while eating my burger and fries. I scan the room but see no one staring. But as we leave, a black 1969 Dodge Charger peels away. I freeze, immediately thinking of Niffin, though I didn't see a driver—or a lack of one. I climb into the station wagon, rattled, and steer us back to the interstate as Mom sightsees obliviously.

That night, we're exhausted and fall asleep quickly. I dream I'm in a cave in the Grand Canyon, facing giants with blackish-brown skin, straight fine hair, high cheekbones, and wide faces—around fifteen feet tall. The men wear Egyptian-style shendyts, shirtless; the women are adorned in colorful sheath dresses. Their leader, a shorter, older woman with white-fringed black curls, speaks kindly, smiling. She tells me the others distrust me, fearing I'll reveal their hidden spot. As I leave, she waves from the cave mouth, men behind her glaring with menace.

I wake to Mom getting dressed. I mention my dream about Egyptian giants in the Grand Canyon. She looks puzzled and says she dreamt of a pyramid near an Arizona gas station. We laugh at our oddly matched dreams, but the coincidence unsettles me—what are the odds?

CHAPTER 22

*W*e roll into Texas, and I feel a little letdown at the flat expanse, grass yellowing as we head west. I stop for gas and a soda. The bottles are huge, proving that, indeed, everything's bigger here. Mom's weary from driving and suggests a day or two of rest. We reach Dallas and book two nights at a hotel, planning to unwind tomorrow with a stroll through the mall.

I'm eager to swim at the hotel while we rest. As dusk falls, we pull off the interstate. Mom checks in while I park and haul our suitcases toward the lobby. She guides me to a room right beside it—clean and neat, with double beds under purple-and-gold floral comforters, purple curtains over light yellow sheers, a desk, and a TV on a dresser. The only mirror's in the bath-room vanity.

We turn in early, thinking about breakfast. I drift off and dream I'm approaching an old adobe church in a desert sea, painted white inside and out. I step into a lobby, then a hallway with a door to the left. It opens to a sanctuary, an alcove along the wall holding a hand-carved wooden podium, its uneven surfaces showing faint tool marks.

To the right of the podium lies a small in-ground baptism pool. The room's filled with dark, aged wooden pews, untreated by modern standards, and a white ceiling to keep it cool. I notice there are no windows as my gaze shifts to the pool. Suddenly, I see a cave beneath it, leading to an empty swimming pool where giant men in trunks sit, facing me. Then I'm outside; the church fades, replaced by a modern school on a bustling city block. Time has erased the church, but the dream carries a heavy sadness, like someone's memory aching for meaning.

I wake facing the window, the curtains parted slightly to let in some light. A dark figure is peering through the gap, staring hard until it sees me stir. It backs off, walking back and forth past the window. I rise and peek out, hearing a car engine rev. Headlights flare in the lot as a black 1969 Dodge Charger pulls away.

I nearly collapse, my heart racing, and glance at Mom, who's still asleep. Fear grips me—I've let prayer and Bible reading slip. I pray for protection, repenting, vowing to restart my routine tomorrow.

I wake up groggy and tired. After eating breakfast in the motel, Mom asks the desk clerk for directions to the mall. I'm too exhausted to drive or pray well, so she takes the wheel. At the mall, I wander alone for a breather, trying to pray but losing focus. A towering woman—maybe six-foot-seven—catches my eye. Dressed in black, she somehow always keeps her back to me while she browses the stores.

She flickers in and out of sight. Mom rushes over to me and asks, "Did you see her?" She also mentions a cloaked man with a covered face and a wand. "He lunged at me in the crowd, muttering in some guttural, clicking language," she spits out, "but he vanished when I dodged him."

She's speaking loudly, and I'm worried people might think she's unhinged. "Shh," I say, trying to calm her down. "Let's talk about it when we get back to the hotel."

She walks around a bit more, and then we talk about what we want for dinner. After we eat, we head home for the rest of the night. I swim while she watches TV.

We leave the next morning, and I realize I barely prayed yesterday. As we drive, I picture cowboys on horseback in old Texas garb instead of focusing on God. I dislike the way I'm drifting from Him, and I don't understand why it's happening.

The landscape shifts to brown, dirt-covered hills as we hit El Paso. I love the western architecture flashing by on the interstate. Past El Paso, everything stays the same—no New Mexico sign yet. The gas stations start to thin out, some thirty miles apart, amid low mountains and high hills.

When we get a chance, we stop for gas and diet sodas. I browse the station, grabbing snacks since eateries are growing scarce.

I find myself drawn to the desert, feeling at home, as if I'd been happy here long ago. A sign confirms we've hit New Mexico, and I pull into a cute light-blue adobe welcome center with a courtyard and matching fountain. Pink mountains and grassy fields come into view as I drive on.

Mom wants to stop in Santa Fe for the night. I'm unsure what to expect, but the adobe homes and churches echo my church dream—though that one was white and in a harsher desert. It must've been Arizona. I can't help but adore Santa Fe's adobe charm anyway. Mom suggests we come back here for a vacation sometime.

We cross into Arizona, greeted by chaotic boulders strewn along the interstate. I pull into the welcome center and park, waiting for Mom in a sitting area, watching the land and people. After a bit we hit the road again. It's routine by now: lunch a few hours later, then back on the highway. I start to feel Mom's looming departure—she's been good company.

A couple hours more, and we reach the college, which has a working film studio attached to it. We pass sets on the left, then colonial brick buildings—over a century old, according to the pamphlet—scattered yet shaded by Desert Ironwood, Desert Willow, and Arizona Ash trees, dotted with benches.

I park in the guest area, and we head inside to find my dorm check-in. It's four buildings away—small campus. A lady at the desk directs us to my building, a well-kept relic with high ceilings, a winding white staircase behind a glossy light-brown circular desk, and four big windows to the right.

I opt to leave the car and walk, the trees providing cooling shade. A circular area with benches is on the left. Ahead, I see an older Native American man with long black hair and a turquoise necklace striding toward a classroom building. He glances at me with an odd expression.

I brush it off as we reach the second-to-last building, the fifth on campus. Its colonial porch boasts white pillars and a black metal chandelier over oak double doors. Inside, a worn oak staircase rises ahead, flanked by a dining room to the left—dark green floral wallpaper, cherry wood tables, green-padded chairs—and a sitting room to the right—pink Victorian couches, cherry coffee tables, eighteen armchairs in rows, gold chandelier, and Greek-themed wallpaper I can't place.

Mom wants to see my room, so we climb to the second door on the left. It's got a twin bed with a tan comforter sporting black movie camera and clipboard designs, an oak veneer desk and dresser with a small mirror, a sink with a medicine cabinet, and a brick-walled window with matching curtains. A black mini fridge sits between the desk and dresser. There's no closet—Mom suggests a portable one for the left wall. She sees a rotary phone on the desk, prompting her to call Dad and fill him in on dorm details. "How do you like Arizona so far?" he asks.

"I love it," I reply. He sounds pleased.

Mom's missing Dad—the midday call's a clear sign. She suggests lunch. I note that we've still got to unload, but she brushes it off, sensing the trip's coming to an end. We eat in a small town. I have a taco salad, while she tries the steak fajitas.

The restaurant's a brown adobe with colorful bird-and-flower tiles, with photos of western actors on the walls. I start to feel a little homesick. Only my parents tie me back home now, with Cherie wrapped up in Ryan. I'll enjoy their visits and trips home.

Mom hunts for a portable closet at a local store. I pick a tan one with black wild horse, cowboy boot, and sheriff badge silhouettes. "Looks a little more Texas than Arizona," she teases.

Back at the dorm, we unload my stuff. Mom's allowed to use a guest room while helping me set up. I spot a church near the restaurant for Sunday—Mom'll be gone by then, flying out Saturday. I'll be solo soon.

Mom fetches some leftover items, saying there's a huge black dog with a square head by the car. She drags me out to see, but it's gone. Instead I see that Native American man walking by, heading to the guys' dorm. Embarrassed again, I tense as she rants. He stops, introduces himself as Lance—a teacher living in the dorm during the semester, home on the Navajo Reservation the rest of the time. Mom warms to him, pivoting from the dog to chat about the school year and campus. We talk briefly, say goodbye to Lance, and finish setting up my room.

CHAPTER 23

A few days pass, and now I'm driving Mom to the airport. A quiet sadness settles over me, a disconnect I can't shake. I'll miss her quirky rants—often about nothing, yet always entertaining in their wild energy. I catch her gazing out the passenger window, and I know she'll feel the ache of this goodbye too.

We're a couple of hours from the airport, winding through a vast, lonely desert. My eyes drift to a saguaro cactus standing tall against the horizon. Its stark beauty captivates me, though it feels alien compared to the familiar embrace of trees. Mom seems taken with Arizona's rugged charm as well, her face soft with admiration.

Silence stretches between us, thick with unspoken thoughts. I wonder about my first semester—new faces I'll meet, lessons I'll learn—but Mom is likely worrying about me, thinking about life back home without my presence, all while soaking in the desert's expanse. The drive drags on, the heat shimmering off the pavement in waves. The stillness is both peaceful and faintly menacing.

Mom brushes sweat and dust from her forehead, mentioning that she'd love a diet fountain drink. After a while, a gas station emerges from the haze. She heads inside to grab us both one, and I stay in the car, a prickling sense of being watched creeping up my spine. I scan the empty lot but find no one.

We pull back onto the road, drinks in hand, when that watched feeling grows more urgent. Out of nowhere, a wet, reeking mass—like soaked cat food piled on newspaper—splats across the windshield, blanketing nearly all of it. I flick on the wipers, smearing it into a gritty mess that slowly clears. Mom shrieks for me to stop, terrified something's in the road, and lunges for the wheel, spilling soda everywhere. I brake hard, wrestling the wipers to clear the gunk, and come to a halt, residue still clinging to the car's edges.

Mom leaps out, circles the wagon, and launches into a frantic tirade about how this could've happened. My focus snaps upward as a massive black crow with iridescent blue-green eyes soars overhead, staring down at me. I stand frozen in the middle of this deserted road, gunk-streaked car behind me, Mom drenched in soda, hysterically claiming I'd have died without her here.

At the airport, Mom waves goodbye before heading to her terminal, in a brighter mood after changing into fresh clothes from her suitcase. She must miss Dad, and I'm sure she's eager to get home after our chaotic drive. I force an optimistic smile, hiding my worry as I watch her go.

Before returning to campus, I find a car wash to scrub the car clean. On the drive back, I switch on the radio, letting the music fill the quiet as I pray softly. I resolve to attend church Sunday and commit to daily prayer and Bible reading, no matter how busy life gets.

Back at the dorms, hunger nudges me to check the dining room. I enter my building, turn left through the open French doors, and spot a plate of chocolate-chip cookies and brownies on a table. As I reach for one, a towering figure approaches—pale as moonlight, with long white hair and huge black owl eyes, draped in a flowing white robe. His gaze radiates disdain. I look away, then back, but he's gone, a faint breeze brushing past as my napkin flutters to the floor. I grab my food and hurry to my room.

Tonight, I sleep with the light on, rattled by the day's events. I wake to footsteps echoing down the hall and glance at my clock—10:10 p.m. I haven't slept long, but other students must be returning for tomorrow's first classes.

Morning arrives with the sound of more footsteps and the chiming of my alarm. I dress for my first day in a floral sundress, tan sandals, and a light white cardigan for chilly classrooms, pulling my hair into a high ponytail. Brushing my teeth, I notice my left lateral incisor is sitting higher than usual—odd, like my irregular periods over the years. I'll keep an eye on it.

Downstairs, chatter spills from the dining room on the right as I descend the front stairs. I'm eager to meet people and make friends. Inside, girls in jeans and t-shirts laugh over breakfast, some eyeing me briefly before looking away. I smile, heading to the buffet for bacon, scrambled eggs, and orange juice from a table lined with pitchers—apple, cranberry, orange—plus utensils and napkins.

I eat alone, feeling out of place but holding steady. After clearing my plate, I head to my first class in the building behind administration. It mirrors the first—plain sitting area with four hunter-green Victorian couches in a circle under a gold chandelier, white wallpaper with red roses climbing leafy stems, and two long windows with heavy green curtains pulled aside.

My classroom's down the left hallway, third room on the right. Nerves mix with excitement as I step in—rows of light-brown desks face a teacher perched on hers, dressed in burgundy slacks and a cream floral blouse, her light brunette hair falling straight down. She watches me enter without a smile. I take the desk nearest the door, eager to finish and grab my textbooks.

The class ends, and I move on to my next one, two doors down—film production. Lance sits at the desk against the back wall, smiling warmly in light jeans and a plaid shirt with rolled-up sleeves. I sit in the front, at ease as he dives into the syllabus with humor and energy.

I'm so caught up in Lance's engaging style I barely notice my classmates. After the class, students swarm him, so I head to my last two classes—math and science—then to the bookstore upstairs in administration. It's a bustling maze of shelves and chatter. I find my books and spot Judith, from English, at one of three circular checkout registers.

I mention recognizing her from class, but she only half-listens, ringing me up. When I ask about her job, she says students can apply, especially for financial aid, and points me to administration. I pay and head to my room to read, but hunger strikes at 5:40 p.m. Downstairs, I see Judith at dinner. "Hi!" I say.

She replies coolly. I grab spaghetti and meatballs with baguette, eating alone, realizing I've neglected prayer and scripture. I promise myself I'll go to church Wednesday.

Back in my room, I study until bedtime. Next morning, with no classes, I plan to go to the administration office and ask about jobs. Mom's sending $100 monthly for essentials, but I need income to explore the West and fill the time. It seems unlikely that I'll find any friends here. I study, eat, and visit administration. Turns out that set-building jobs are open at the studio. They tell me to talk about it with Lance tomorrow.

As I return to my dorm, that watched feeling washes over me again. No one's behind me, but it lingers in my room. A strange energy resists my urge to pray or read scripture. I give in and sleep without either.

I wake groggy, blaming my poor sleep on nervousness related to the new school. I can hear Judith whispering in the hall about me talking to a man at midnight. But I was alone, asleep. Mom heard something similar back home. I suddenly wonder why I even applied here. Was I under Niffin's sway? Why this college? Exhausted, I push through my classes.

After my last class, I nap, miss church by oversleeping, and wake to darkness, feeling awful. In the dining room, I find to-go boxes—meatloaf, green beans, mac and cheese, cornbread—plus iced tea and lemonade. I heat one, grab some lemonade, and exit. I see a robed man with long hair, all in black, his owl eyes glaring and a neon-red stripe running down his face like a war mark. He vanishes when I blink. Shaken, I sleep with the light on, vowing to go to church on Sunday.

In the morning, I notice that my incisor's shifted even more, and I've inexplicably gained weight. Self-conscious, I withdraw further, deciding to focus on school and ask Lance about the job Friday.

When Friday comes, campus feels empty. There's no classes, and many students gone. At the studio, crews laugh while building sets. I see Lance and wave. He's busy but says I can apply at administration for an interview Tuesday. I fill out the form there and turn it in.

I need an escape, so I plan to visit nearby Native American ruins over the weekend. Back in my room, I pray and read scripture, feeling lighter, excited for Tuesday and my trip.

Saturday, I rise at 8:00 a.m., grabbing banana muffins, milk, and orange juice from breakfast—the weekend spread is a lot sparser than that on weekdays. I make a mental note to save Friday to-go meals next time. When I get in my car, I take out the maps Mom gave me and write down the directions to the ruins, thrilled my first week's finally done.

The desert looks beautiful today. The drive is long, with few stops along the way. As I'm driving, I see a wolf with glowing blue-green eyes blocking the road, staring confidently at me as I slow to pass. It watches me go, unmoving, until it fades from my rearview mirror.

I reach the turnoff for the ruins, struck by their similarity to my dream. There are cliff dwellings ahead, with a modern road to a visitor center and restaurant on the right. The Navajo didn't build these, a sign reads; Hopi ancestors, the Hisatsinom, did. Tours cost extra, so I admire the dwellings from afar, all carved into the cliffs. I eat at the restaurant, alone, unlike in my dream with Mom. Is she tied to Niffin somehow? I stop at a little picnic area, scoop dirt into a bag—feeling a strange urge to connect to this place— then drive back, hiding my odd keepsake so no one sees me.

CHAPTER 24

On Sunday morning, I drive to a church in a small town near campus. It's a plain cream-stucco building with heavy dark-wood double doors, no front windows, but vibrant stained-glass ones along the sides. Inside, a foyer opens to a hallway with bathrooms and classrooms to the left and a sanctuary straight ahead, with dark wood pews flanking a matching podium. The pastor and a few congregants greet me warmly, curious about my life at film school.

I notice a striking guy ahead to my left—light brown hair, blue eyes, tall and lean, with high cheekbones and a bright smile. His perfect teeth flash as he chats with friends. There's no girlfriend in sight. I'd love to talk to him, but shyness holds me back.

Back at the dorm, I wish for nearby escapes—a bookstore, coffee shop, anything. Then I recall a grocery store close by. If I get the job on Tuesday, I could buy tea and snacks. The thought of being able to leave when I want to makes me even more eager to start working.

Monday flies by, and the classes are decent. I finish some assignments in my room, read scripture, pray, and sleep. In the morning I hear Judith's voice outside again. She's claiming I smoke in my room—against policy. I bolt up, spotting cigarettes on my desk, a faint smoky haze lingering. Oddly, the curtains and bed smell clean. I air the room out, rattled.

Something's entering my room—I need more than locks. Maybe a camera from film school, or I can buy one with money I make from the job. My mood sours, and I feel irritation and discouragement rising in me, but prayer and scripture push it down, at least for a while. I steel myself and push through.

I pray about my interview. I can overhear Judith talking about me again. She says I'm weird and claims I have a secret boyfriend who stays over. I'm not sure what to do. Confronting her risks exposing the cigarettes and the smoke. She's got no proof, so I let her talk, wondering how I ever ended up at this college.

When she's gone, I dress for the interview—jeans, a black floral blouse, black sandals, a black bead bracelet. I don't have earrings. Mom wouldn't let me get piercings until I was sixteen, and by then I'd lost interest. I lock my door and head to Lance's classroom.

My stomach's churning as I arrive. I hope it's not obvious. Lance welcomes me warmly, asking about my experience. I mention helping at my parents' store. He grins, says I'm a quick learner, and offers me a set-building job starting Wednesday. He'll have paperwork tomorrow after class for the employment office, and I'll need two forms of ID.

I leave buoyed, craving a celebration. With $11 left, I hit the grocery store and grab a small chocolate cake—on sale and expiring tomorrow—and a case of store-brand diet soda for my mini fridge. I'll surprise Mom and Dad about the job later after I make sure it's working out. I know once I tell them they'll expect me to be independent and stop sending my allowance.

The cashier is the cute guy from church. Nervous, I check out. He smiles politely, scans my items, and says, "See you soon." I'm both giddy and a little disappointed at the lack of conversation. He barely notices me, and why would he? Well, cake still excites me.

Back at the dorm, I grab a to-go container and utensils from the dining room, but I see three shadowy figures through the frosted glass of the French doors—two adults, one small like a child. I hesitate, then the smallest turns, calling my name in a girl's voice, twice. Chilled, I retreat upstairs.

In my room, I dig out emergency plastic utensils, cutting the cake on its plastic tray. I test the soda, but it's still warm. I wait thirty minutes, then return to the dining room, which is now open. Judith smirks mischievously as I grab milk cartons, salad plates, and utensils, heading back to enjoy my victory properly.

After I finish eating the cake, I head downstairs for spaghetti. When I'm done, I head back and finish some assignments. I feel accomplished but lonely—missing Mom, Dad, even Cherie a bit, and Janis most of all. I'll get a dog someday.

The semester races by and it's time for finals. I bond with Lance and the studio crew—mostly juniors and seniors—learning about set design, lighting, and cameras. I thrive in the ever-shifting chaos of movie sets, loving the constant change.

Lance, kind and encouraging, offers me a spot on a post-finals tour to Monument Valley through the college. I haven't made winter break plans with my parents, although it would be nice to visit them for Christmas. I sign up for the tour; I can cancel if I have to.

After work, I call Mom and ask about Christmas. She suggests that they visit me this year, and maybe I can come home next year. I'm thrilled at the thought of them coming. Despite my crew and Lance, I'm still lonely here.

The following day, Lance pulls me aside at work, looking uneasy. I brace for bad news. Am I getting fired? Instead, he tells me about a huge crow with blue-green eyes in a tree yesterday—only he saw it. That night, he dreamt of fishing on a lake. The water churned, and a house-sized thunderbird rose from the depths, screeching "Bernadette." A shadowy face watched, radiating malice.

"In some tribes, thunderbirds signal protection," he says. "I believe I have been tasked to shield you from something deadly."

I'd rather be fired than hunted by a dark entity. Stunned, I say I'm unsure what to make of it. As I turn, he asks me about talking shadows. I freeze, recalling all those childhood whispers. He calls them evil Navajo witches, generational stalkers.

"Can we talk about it later?" I ask quietly. "I need to get back to work."

Lance watches me all day, genuinely worried. Back in my room, a fierce energy blocks my attempts at prayer and scripture. I give in, resolving to try again tomorrow. I'm still shaken by Lance's words, sensing worse things ahead.

Sleep comes, but I'm awakened by a girl's frantic cries for her mother. I hear pounding on my door, but when I open it the hall's empty, a black strand of hair with a blue ribbon on the floor. I lock the door, drag my desk against it as a barrier, and pray for an hour until the fear fades. I finally drift off to sleep with the light on.

The next day, Lance shares his own odd night before I can speak— watching from the porch of the men's dorm, he saw a black figure speed toward the building and then vanish. In a dream, a stout, dark-haired man in a taxi sought my hand in marriage. Lance refused, sensing evil beneath his charm. The man insisted, claiming me as Nora's replacement—or my family stays cursed.

I'm stunned, unsure how to respond. I tell him about the girl's cries in the night.

"Ah, Navajo witches are able to replay the sounds of their last victims," he says. "But who's Nora?"

"She's my great-grandmother from Arizona, married to my French great-grandfather."

Lance theorizes that this man—Niffin—jilted and angered by Nora's remarriage, is demanding a wife from her line. So now I'm his target. He warns me that the entity could even kill me. He vows to help me, though we're both unsure what to do. I leave feeling defeated yet grateful for Lance and God, trusting in divine protection from Niffin.

CHAPTER 25

I go to bed early, sinking into a deep sleep, only to jolt upright, my heart racing, unsure why. As I settle back down, my dorm lock clicks open. I look, but no one's there. The door's still shut, reminding me of the eerie nights back at home.

A man's voice calls my name, faint at first, then clear. I lie still, hoping it's a dream, until I hear footsteps getting closer—someone testing if I'm awake. I lunge for my lamp, flooding the room with light, but find it empty.

In the morning, I discover that my left incisor is higher still and I've gotten even heavier despite unchanged habits. My self-doubt grows deeper each day.

I craft a plan to defeat Niffin—prayer and scripture daily, no excuses, church every Sunday and Wednesday, the Lord's Prayer each morning:

Our Father, which art in heaven,
Hallowed be thy Name.
Thy Kingdom come.
Thy will be done on earth,
As it is in heaven.
Give us this day our daily bread.
And forgive us our debts,

As we forgive our debtors.
And lead us not into temptation,
But deliver us from evil.
For thine is the kingdom,
The power and the glory, For ever and ever.
Amen

I vow to thank God for each day, to break any covenants made in dreams known or unknown, and to praise Him for every purchase. I'll pray over meals, my groceries, and my drives.

Trusting God's voice proves toughest. When He nudges me down a path, I sometimes resist, only to regret it. Yet I grow closer to Him every day, feeling lighter over time. Church becomes routine. I often see that cute guy —kind, but uninterested. I remain friendly, hoping for connection, trusting God's timing for love.

Finals end, and Christmas break looms. Mom and Dad opt to stay home with Cherie and Ryan, something to do with Ryan's store training. I feel hurt—Cherie hasn't called once to check on me or ask about school, a stark change from better days. Mom promises they'll visit in the summer. I agree, masking my resentment at the loneliness I feel here, a choice I made yet can't shake.

At work, Lance announces an opening for a camera operator for a TV show filming at the studio. Elated, I grab an application from a table near the set entrance, fill it out, and hand it to him the next day. He smiles, saying it'll be a few weeks before any decision is made. I pray ceaselessly for it.

That night, feeling content, I fall asleep quickly but wake with a start when I hear a man's voice calling my name twice, distinctly. There are footsteps outside my door, the light flickering beneath it as if someone's pacing. I freeze, waiting it out, willing it to go away.

I drift off again, and in my dream that cute church guy is sword-fights a cloaked figure. He loses, and falls with a fatal wound into shallow water, staring up at me. He decays, forgotten, a haunting image I can't escape until I wake in the morning. But the feeling of being watched is strong. I rise instead of trying to sleeping anymore.

I faithfully go on prayer walks every day. I started even before I hatched the plan to defeat Niffin, but now they're unmissable. Time flies by, and I eagerly await news about the job.

A letter slips under my door. It's a rejection from Lance, sent privately, hoping I'm not too crushed. I am though, discouraged and disappointed.

As I start to pray later, a fierce energy tries to stop me, rebelling against God—sin's fine, it whispers, given my lot. I stand firm, praying it away.

I need air, so I head to the grocery store for a treat, praying that cute cashier's absent—I still don't even know his name. I'm in luck, and he's not there. I grab a candy bar and diet soda. When I go back outside, I see a black 1969 Dodge Charger idling, its engine revving. A shadowy arm dangles a cigarette from the window as it creeps past, taunting me, daring me to look. Bravely, I step closer, but then I falter. I'm afraid yet curious to see Niffin's face. The car speeds off, stops, and skids sharply, the passenger door creaking ajar. I see the gleaming black leather interior, but there's no one's inside. The engine roars—an invitation to get in! I freeze. The Charger peels out, leaving a trail of burnt rubber. A wave of relief washes over me as it goes, and I turn to see if anyone else has seen what happened. No one's outside but me.

I re-enter the store, grab my soda and Snickers, pay, and head back to my room to dive into scripture and prayer.

The following day, Lance invites the whole crew to his place near the Navajo reservation for Christmas. He says there are two hogans, one for girls and one for guys, on land he owns nearby. We'll leave December 23rd and return the 27th. It sounds perfect since campus will be shut down and my parents aren't coming. There'll be a New Year's party on campus after that. I'm relieved not to be alone.

We'll swap small gifts—$20 limit—plus some extras for all. Lance stays on campus during the semester, his sister minding his reservation home. I don't know what to expect besides a Christmas tree, but I'm eager to go.

Most students will be gone for the holiday. I pack for the trip, excited yet clueless about the reservation. I send cash to Mom, Dad, Cherie, and Ryan for Christmas. They're all so picky anyway. I'll have to do my secret Santa shopping soon.

The studio's shutting down soon; just one week until the holiday break. I help finish a set for a new show about a desert diner, the Lunar Eclipse, with odd guests and quirky mysteries. It's got a 1950s vibe, complete with green-blue checkered floors, dark blue booths, green tables, a steel soda fountain, walls with galaxy-themed murals, and a starry ceiling with twinkling lights. I love the comedic chaos.

Lance says only four are coming to his place, so we nix the secret Santa in favor of small group gifts. We finish the set, and I savor both the process and the result.

Two days until departure, we opt for separate cars over a bus—less company, true, but it's fine. Campus becomes very quiet with students leaving for the holidays. I consider getting a tree for the dorm, but it probably would just make me feel even lonelier.

Back at my room, I see a sticky note on my door saying I have a package in the administration office. I rush over before the staff leave and show it to the secretary. She fetches a brown-paper parcel from Mom. I'll open it on Christmas Day.

The day before leaving for Lance's, I buy holiday chocolates, cookies, and apple and pumpkin pies with long expiration dates from the grocery store—safe, generous gifts.

When morning comes, I load my car, carefully setting the pies in last. That watched feeling returns as I carry them out, but I shake it off, setting them on the passenger seat. Excited for Christmas and the reservation, I gas up, grab a diet soda, and head out, the desert's beauty now familiar yet still enchanting.

Day fades as I near Lance's land, spotting hogans before his two-story cabin—wooden, unlike the local stucco or adobe I'm used to. I park beside other cars, scanning his property. Two old hogans sit out back. I grab the pies, ring the bell, and Lance ushers me in. His sister's there, too, smiling as she takes the pies. Two crew guys are chatting inside. I see that one's missing—maybe he canceled. I'll ask later, but I'm eager to explore the hogans first.

The living room is sprawling, with oak floors and paneling, plaid couches, a stone fireplace with a wall-mounted TV, and a towering Christmas tree covered with red and green ornaments, framed by big windows. Ahead, I see the kitchen with oak cabinets, an island with copper pans overhead, and a cozy eating nook. A long, oak-lined hallway stretches right to where the bedrooms are located.

Lance's sister, Enola, introduces herself. "What a lovely name," I say sincerely.

She smiles as the phone rings, her tone shifting from light to grave. I feign disinterest, unsure who's on the line.

We tour the hogans as Lance and Enola discuss Navajo life. She pulls him aside, a serious expression on her face. I tune it out. The girls' hogan is a circular earth dome, with a wooden door jutting to the east. Inside, lumber beams fan out like the ribs of a log cabin, supporting the dome. There's a modern wood heater replacing the old fire pit, its smokestack sealed. Rugs define spaces: oak living room to the left, dining table and cabinet ahead, and bed and desk to the right. Enola tells us the guys get this one and they'll sleep on air beds, using the shower and restroom in the house. We skip the other hogan, returning for Enola's dinner—burgers, fries, Navajo bread, and apple pie. I can sense she's hiding something.

Later, Enola offers me the guest room in the house. I mask my disappointment—the hogans sounded fun—and accept. We retire, and I'm glad for the missing guy because it means there'll be a gift for Enola.

Sleep eludes me in the cherry-wood guest room. The blinds are open to let light in, and I can see stripes of light on the wall. But then there's something else. I see a tall, horned figure with a square jaw pass outside. Minutes later, the lock on my door clicks, and the door creaks open and then shuts. I look, but nothing's there. I black out, my head hitting the pillow.

Morning comes, and I wake confused, a fresh bruise above my left knee, the desk chair shifted as if someone has been sitting in it. It's Christmas Eve, so I get dressed, realizing that I won't be able to make a long-distance call to my family.

Enola cooks pancakes, bacon, and eggs as we lounge by the tree. It's a warm morning, and after breakfast Lance drives us around the reservation. It's a lot poorer than I expected, and the locals are pretty unfriendly to outsiders. I'm grateful for the glimpse, though he keeps it brief.

Back home, Enola's prepared a wonderful Christmas Eve lunch—ham, sweet potato and green bean casseroles, and rolls, topped off with pumpkin pie. She's prepping turkey for tomorrow. We go on another drive after, this time to the desert near New Mexico. The vistas are absolutely stunning, and we don't return until after dark. When we do, it's clear Enola's not happy about the time.

There's a new guest, Chooli, waiting there, a local who's close to Enola. She's standoffish despite my smile, eyeing me oddly. Finding her disinterested, I talk with the others, forgetting about her altogether until she says something that piques my interest. She says that tied-up coyotes were spotted yesterday—Navajo witch signs. That's why Enola kept me inside, not alone in a hogan. Chooli looks at me suspiciously. I can't tell if she thinks I'm a witch or if I'm the reason one would be creeping around here.

Chooli hands Enola a jar of gray ashes, whispering, then glares at me and leaves. Enola pivots, trying to rescue the evening with a Christmas movie and cookies. Lance, edgy, eyes the windows. I can see a shotgun resting by the door. Something's near, they know; the crew guys, oblivious, enjoy the film. I envy their peace.

After the first move, everyone decides to watch another, pushing the gift exchange off until tomorrow. I feel the prickle of being watched. It's coming from outside, and I start scanning the windows like Lance.

Sleepiness hits us all. Lance and Enola watch the guys head out to the hogan, while I had to the guest room for the night. In my room, I hear whispers guttural, clicking chants coming from the hall. I crack the door open and see a dark figure standing just outside, its back turned. It must be Lance. "What are you doing?" I ask.

He shifts at my voice but stays silent. "It's not funny," I pout, shutting the door. But before I can get back into bed, I hear knocking.

I open the door slowly. The dark figure is there, right against the door, but turned sideways so I can't see its face. The dread of being watched washes over me. I try to shut the door, but a hand with long, pointy nails holds it open. It's not Lance, it's Niffin! I scream as he yanks the door wide, dragging me down the hall toward the front of the house.

I hear a commotion as Lance and Enola awaken. I do my best to stall Niffin, my feet scraping the oak floors, as Enola yells for ash-dipped bullets. I scream for God, resisting Niffin's grip with all my strength. Lance grabs the shotgun, loading it as Enola pries me free. Two blasts hit Niffin. I suddenly remember the legend about calling witches by their real name. "Niffivempier!" I shout. And in a flash, he's gone.

Enola flips on the lights, revealing blood and bits of decaying flesh on the floor. I bolt outside, Lance and Enola trailing. Faint voices draw me around the house—two robed figures loom over a rotted corpse. One looks like Nora. Instinctively, I know it must be her daughter with Niffin. The man is his brother. They fade away as Lance and Enola reach me.

After a long pause, Enola tells me that some say you can kill a Navajo witch with silver, ash, or names—no one's sure, and the secrets are closely guarded. She insists I sleep on the living room couch with her, so she can guard me against Niffin's return.

When I finally fall asleep, I dream I'm in an airport with that man I saw at the grocery store man all those years ago, checking in. He's worried, glancing at his watch. I turn to the agent, and when I look back, he's gone. I go to look for him, but I'm with family. I try to call him but get no answer. Customer service can't page him.

My family waits on me as I use the restroom, but they're also gone when I emerge. I trek through the endless airport, and I'm told I can go into a room and take a nap until my flight takes off. Inside, Mom's on a hospital bed in what looks like a delivery room. I accidentally knock a paper off of a nurse's desk. It falls into a bucket of water, causing the lower two-thirds blur, but the top is still visible. I recognize it. It's the contract I signed with Niffin's contract, now void. The curse has been lifted—a miracle from God.

When I wake in the morning, the guys join us, evidently unfazed by the events of last night. Lance is annoyed and asks if they were scared or concerned about the shots. They're surprised and say they heard nothing.

The house feels friendlier, safe. The scent of Enola's pumpkin pancakes, bacon, eggs, turkey, and spices fill the house. We swap modest gifts: socks, peppermint tea, lotion, gloss, bark, gum, pumpkin tea, a candle. I fetch Mom's package and open it. Inside's a $50 card, jewelry, and heirlooms, including a turquoise heart locket with half a ruby inside, once Nora's, part Navajo.

Enola looks stricken. She tears up and pulls out an identical locket—with the other half of the ruby. Nora was her great-grandmother's twin, the first Enola, for whom she was named. Nora's later kids explain our age gap; her first, with a Navajo man here, vanished from record. Lance says that Niffin, furious about Nora remarrying, must have sought to end or claim her line. That's the curse I'd been fighting all my life!

I pray Niffin's really gone, trusting God's salvation and grateful for this reunion with Nora's kin. It's a miracle I'll share with my parents, proof of divine power that I'll never forget.

www.ingramcontent.com/pod-product-compliance
Lightning Source LLC
Chambersburg PA
CBHW051839020726
47502CB00005B/1868